T0194967

LOVE
BURNS
BRIGHT

LOVE BURNS BRIGHT

A LIFETIME OF LESBIAN ROMANCE

EDITED BY
RADCLYFFE

Copyright © 2013 by Radclyffe.

All rights reserved. Except for brief passages quoted in newspaper, magazine, radio, television, or online reviews, no part of this book may be reproduced in any form or by any means, electronic or mechanical, including photocopying or recording, or by information storage or retrieval system, without permission in writing from the publisher.

Published in the United States by Cleis Press, Inc.,
221 River Street, 9th Floor, Hoboken, NJ 07030

Printed in the United States.
Cover design: Scott Idleman/Blink
Cover photograph: Granefelt, Lena/Getty Images
Text design: Frank Wiedemann

First Edition.
10 9 8 7 6 5 4 3 2 1

Trade paper ISBN: 978-1-62778-000-1
E-book ISBN: 978-1-62778-013-1

"A Story about Sarah" © Cheyenne Blue, Lesbian Lust, Cleis Press, 2010; "Waiting for the Harvest" © Sommer Marsden, Eat Me, Pretty Things Press, 2010; "Heartfirst" © Kiki DeLovely, Best Lesbian Erotica 2012, Cleis Press, 2011.

Contents

INTRODUCTION

Romance fiction is the largest-selling segment of trade fiction, outdistancing mystery, erotica, historical fiction, sci-fi/fantasy and every permutation of every other sub-genre. Why are romances so popular? Easy to read? Easy to write? Not too taxing—fast, quick, disposable? Every one of these reasons has been given to explain why the reading public loves romance—none are absolutely accurate and each misses the fundamental truth about romance fiction. Romances are stories exploring one of the central aspects of human life—our intimate emotional, spiritual and physical connections with other human beings. Every time I edit a romance anthology, I try to find a definition of romance that encompasses the complexity of intimate human relationships—a Sisyphean task, since romance is so often an experience unique to individual experience. We can all enumerate elements universally common to the romantic experience—the thrill of meeting "the right person"; the breathless anticipation of the first date, the first kiss, the first night of passion; the mind-altering euphoria that infuses our waking moments and often invades our dreams as we experience our fantasies about to come true. But what about love after that first blush of euphoria fades and we move on to the future we so ecstatically envisioned? Romance novels by definition end at the "happily ever after." The reader knows, with confidence and satisfaction, the two lovers will go on to share a future in a committed and passionate relationship. The selections in this anthology tell the rest of the story, depicting the many ways lesbian couples experience love and romance after the honeymoon—celebrating their love, sharing their strengths and sustaining their passion.

Love doesn't always start with a storybook beginning—sometimes it takes a lifetime to find—as in Rebekah Weatherspoon's "Forever Yours, Eileen," where two women wait nearly fifty years to embrace their desire, making the eventual union all the more precious. Sometimes forever is just in the knowing there will always be a next time, as Jay Lawrence's narrator in "Darrell" says about her sometimes lover, forever love:

> Darrell is a butterfly. She lives completely in the present, without regret. I know I can never possess her, I can only seize the day.... Summer can't last forever, but it always returns.

And then there are the relationships which we see every day in our communities, the committed couples living the dream—the house, the job, the in-laws, the kids—stealing moments, creating ways to keep love and passion alive. Their stories show us that indeed, there is romance and eros after the honeymoon. Enjoy these glimpses of love, commitment and forever passion that celebrate not just the beginning of love, but the happily-ever-after and beyond.

Radclyffe, 2013

FOREVER YOURS, EILEEN

Rebekah Weatherspoon

I'm sitting in a Manhattan diner with my grandson June. He's named after me and right now he's driving me nuts. I would have come alone, but I'm waiting for Eileen. It's been fifteen years since we've seen each other, so yes, I'm nervous. Juney offered to be my support today. I wanted to turn him down, but his chatter is distracting me. He came out to me when he was very young. We helped each other, I like to think. He's the right person to have by my side.

He reaches across the table toward the stack of envelopes I've tucked under my arm. I smack his fingers away.

"Ow, Grandma!" He laughs, though.

"You know better than to get all grabby."

"I can't believe you save all of these letters."

It was Mama's idea initially. Keep all the letters, and one day when we're old ladies, we can laugh about them. I'm too anxious to laugh now.

I shrug and gaze out the diner window. I think about the

pages and pages I have in my hands, and there's not a second thought about having a choice in the matter. God wanted me to keep the letters. The letters are what got us here.

"Can I please read one?" June asks.

"Fine, but don't rip it." I reach down to the bottom and pull out the first envelope. There's two letters tucked inside, the first letter I ever wrote to Eileen, and the first letter she ever wrote back.

It's April 1956, and we're driving away from our home. Mama and Daddy fought for weeks over selling the farm. It was the first piece of anything Granddaddy ever owned. Mama was born in that house, but as Daddy has said a whole heap of times, "The South ain't what it should be, and it's time for us to go." Mama's upset because Grandma won't come with us. She's too old for the Klan to bother her, she says. She moves in with our uncle, who says he's not scared enough to walk away from his job in Jackson. Daddy calls him a fool, but he understands. My uncle doesn't have any sons.

I'm only nine, and even though I understand why we're leaving, I cry all the way to Tennessee. Later, after I have three sons of my own I'm finally able to wrap my mind around my parents' decision. You do what you have to do for your children. Daddy can fight for himself, but he doesn't trust his boys in the hands of Jim Crow. All the same, I cry with my head on Fredrick's shoulder all the way across the state line. I already miss Grandma and our dog Mickey. Mr. Hammond bought him with the farm because he's good at chasing small creatures that like to tear up the garden. Most of all, I miss Eileen.

She's my best friend in the world. We met when we were knee-high in Sunday school, and our mamas would joke that it would take the hand of god to pull us little devils apart. The hand of god or my daddy's determination. Mama said I could write Eileen letters. It would be a great way for me to work on my spelling and my penmanship. Plus I'd have my very own pen pal. And that's what I did. The minute we got to Brooklyn I wrote Eileen a letter, not caring a lick about my penmanship.

Dear Eileen, I hate it here. The people are weird. There's no grass and everything smells like gasoline and poop.

My grandson looks up from the paper. He's about to crumple with laughter. "Brooklyn smelled like poop in the fifties?"

"When you're used to fresh air everything in the city smells like poop. Do you want to read the letter or do you want to make fun of me?"

He laughs again. "Sorry. I'll be good."

It takes forever for me to hear back from Eileen, but her first letter is the first bright spot in our move. We come all this way and Fredrick gets beat up on his first day of school. George gets mussed up trying to help him. It takes Daddy forever to find work. Almost four months go by with the five of us living in my cousin's living room. Mama is cleaning rooms at this lousy hotel. She's exhausted every time she comes home, but she's always looking on the bright side. We finally get our own place, and the last day I'm helping Mama pack up our things, the mailman brings Eileen's letter.

Dear Juney, Sorry it took me so long to write back. I was waiting for something juicy to happen so I'd have some news. Nothing happened. Mama said you all were smart to leave. I asked her if we could move to Brooklyn too even though you said it was bad, but she said no.

* * *

"I can't handle how adorable this letter is," my grandson says.

I shrug again. "We were adorable kids."

"Are you nervous?"

"No."

"Well, you look fly, Grandma."

I glance down at my leather jacket and my matching boots. June helped pick out my jeans. He keeps me young. Finally I smile. "Thanks, baby."

"Let me read one more." I fish out the last letter I sent in junior high school. After that Eileen and I both start to mature, and there's things your grandchild doesn't need to know.

I write to her about Mrs. Stein and how she's invited me to take her ballet classes. Mama is wary at first, but after Mrs. Stein explains that her dream of dancing again is what got her through the war, Mama knows I'm in good hands. I hear people aren't so happy about her teaching mixed classes, but no one tries to stop her. I tell Eileen everything I'm learning, all the French terms. I promise I'll show her if we get to see each other again. When she writes back, she promises we will.

She writes me about the etiquette classes they started offering at the church and how her mama is making her go after she caught Eileen wiping her hands on the back of her sister's dress.

Our junior year in high school, Eileen writes me about her first boyfriend. Mama won't let me date. Some of my friends at school have steadies, but I think they are all jokers and my friends are silly for mooning over them. I want to think that maybe Eileen will shed some light on the appeal of liking a boy, but as I read her letter I find something other than curiosity rising in my mind.

It's a strange thing, Juney. I thought it would be different. Clara Winston and her boyfriend are always pawing at each other, but Harry doesn't want to neck or anything. He's going to college in the fall and he wants to be a doctor. I asked why he's not trying to get in my pants, and he said a gentleman waits until he's married. How sweet is that? I think that's why I like him. He's smart and he's going places and he listens to me when I talk. It's not a game of grabby hands when we're together. We did kiss, though. It was nice.

She sounds happy in the letter, and I'm happy for her, but later when I reread those particular pages I realize how jealous I was. I wait a while before I write back. I tell Mama about Eileen's boyfriend. She assures me it won't last. "It's just young love, Juney. He'll move on when he goes off to school."

"But you and Daddy met when you were young," I remind her.

"And I was the only girl around who wasn't bucktoothed or his cousin." She's teasing to make me feel better. When I finally answer Eileen's letter, I ask an obnoxious number of questions about Harry. When she writes back she tells me she's sorry for talking about him so much. I think she means it.

After a time, I finally see Eileen again. I've finished my third year at SUNY and she's finished her third year at Spelman. The government's just sent Fredrick's body back to us from Vietnam. Mama's a mess and she makes George promise he'll dodge if his number comes up. Daddy doesn't argue. I do what I can to hold it together, but I fall apart when I call Eileen. I can't wait for her reply in a letter. She lets me sob in her ear for as long as Daddy will let me be on the phone.

I come unhinged again when she shows up with her daddy at the funeral. She holds my hand the whole time, and I think that's the moment I realize I love her. I can't put it into words yet, but the warmth of her fingers is the first real comfort I've felt since we left Mississippi. I don't want her to leave, but of course she does. Her daddy can only miss so much work.

The following Christmas, Harry proposes to her. She calls me. I convince her that I'm happy for them. We all go down for the wedding that spring. Fredrick's with us too because a year later the war is still going strong and the cloud of his death hasn't lifted. Eileen looks beautiful. I can't keep my eyes off her, and I let the joy of seeing her and the comfort of being home get me through the day. I'm cordial to Harry, genuinely grateful that he does seem like a nice man. On the trip back to New York, I cry again. I tell Mama I miss Fred.

Back in Brooklyn I quickly find that I make a good secretary, but I make an even better dancer. I ask Mrs. Rosenbaum, Mrs. Stein's daughter, if she'll let me teach a class at her studio. She says yes. I meet Walter on the bus one night on my way back from class. He's new to the city from Boston. He likes that I still have traces of my accent. He walks me all the way home one night and many more nights after. He asks Daddy if he can marry me. I beg Daddy to say yes, not because I love Walter, but because I know I'm supposed to. Daddy says yes.

I call Eileen to tell her the news. She tells me she's pregnant. I think we both pretend to be happy for each other. We keep writing to each other. I actually find that her pregnancy mends things I didn't realize were broken. She focuses on the baby now and not Harry or her church friends. I like hearing about her joys and her fears of being a mother. She's too far along to come to our wedding, but I send her a few pictures and she sends us pictures of her baby girl.

After that, our kids are all we talk about.

* * *

It's not a particular movement on the street that catches my eye, it's Eileen. I'd see her anywhere. At any distance, in any crowd. She passes by the window, her daughter and two grandkids in tow. The bell rings on the diner door and I spring to my feet. The introductions are a blur except for the one moment Sandra looks at me. She hates me. Eileen's told me in her letters that she's taken the news the hardest. You'd think it was me that killed her father and not the heart attack.

Even though her upbringing keeps her from saying so, she wishes her mother were anywhere but in this diner with me. It's written all over her face. Still she smiles at June and half smiles at me. I smile back and keep from laying out the truth she doesn't want to hear. I've waited nearly fifty years to be with her mother again. Her attitude is not going to keep us apart.

"Mom, are you settled?" Sandra finally says.

Eileen looks at me with an anxious smile. "Yeah. You kids go on. I'll see you back at the hotel."

Sandra says okay before she turns to June. "We have an extra ticket to *The Lion King*—"

"Just in case these two chickened out?"

I call on all of Jesus to keep from smacking the boy in the back of the head.

Sandra and her kids all chuckle at his joke. "Yes. Would you like to come along?"

"Sure. I know some people. Maybe I can get you backstage." With that June sweeps them out the door with his charm. Sandra glances back one more time before they disappear down the street.

Eileen and I are still standing in the aisle, just looking at each other. We sit, suddenly nervous again when a waitress comes bustling by. It's been a long time. We're both older. We're both grayer, but nothing about either of us has changed.

"You look great, Juney," she finally says.

"So do you."

I ask her about her trip. She confesses that Sandra is still worried. Then she asks to see the letters. There are so many things I want to do. Making love to her being at the top of the list, but I need to give her time. I slide the stack across the table and then I wait. Our coffee comes, and then her salad. I order some fries and pie, and I watch her as she reads.

I had a feeling which letter she was looking for. I've read it over a hundred times, when I was preparing to leave Walter and on so many nights after I found myself alone in a tiny apartment, wishing I had the money to take my youngest baby with me.

It's the letter I wrote before I convinced Walter that we needed a vacation. I told him I wanted the boys to see their Southern roots. I promised him some romance near the swimming hole if it was still there. Really I want to see Eileen. She and Harry are more than happy to have us. Once we arrive and the boys are settled in chasing Eileen's girls all over her yard, and Harry's convinced Walter to play some dominos, Eileen and I set off down her road on our own.

We walk for a while. She tells me about her girls driving her crazy. I tell her about the fast hussies sniffing around my boys now that they've shot up. She gets quiet, though, after a while and then she says, "I was thinking about what you said in your letter about Walter, about it not being him."

"About men in general?"

"Yeah. I think about that sometimes too." We stop walking. I hear crickets everywhere, even the warm air moving around us as I turn to look at Eileen. She looks at the ground.

"I don't...I don't think I have those feelings for Harry anymore."

I hear the words, but they don't make sense. I wrote that letter because I had to put those emotions somewhere before I burst. I think all women have a sense of wanting more or something different. It's in our blood, I think, but we deal with what we're dealt. I expect her to understand a little bit about feeling somewhat trapped or looking at a man after fifteen years and wondering if you can stomach fifteen more because you don't know when you'll ever get a chance to live for yourself. But that part I wrote and didn't take back about men in general? I didn't expect Eileen to understand that.

I try to play it off. "Maybe you just need to get the spark back." I say that foolish thing knowing how phony it sounds. I'm glad she doesn't give up.

"That's not what I mean, Juney. I don't think I feel that way about Harry anymore. Or anyone really. 'Cept you."

Her eyes meet mine. She's open and vulnerable, and I don't know what I'm thinking because we're out in the middle of the road, but I kiss her. The strangest part is not that I'm kissing my best friend, but that she doesn't seem shocked. She's kissing me back, guiding us sightless off the road until my back touches the rough bark of a tall pine. The scratching sensation through my shirt brings me back down to earth and I realize this kiss is real, not something I've made up in my mind. I know now that I've been kissing the wrong lips all along.

We break apart and I see that Eileen is just as scared as I am. She takes a step back and touches her lips. But that fear isn't disgust or shame. It's a realization. It's the truth.

"How do we do this?" I ask, because I know now for sure it's not Walter who I want to be with. It's not men at all.

"I don't think we can."

My heart sinks, but I understand how she feels. It's more than this feeling between us. It's our babies. It's these two men who've given us everything. Walter who's worked so we can afford for me to teach dance for next to nothing, and Harry who allows Eileen to stay home with the girls. It's friends and family. For Eileen it's church and community. How do we turn our backs on that?

I grab her and kiss her again. It's a final kiss. At least it is for a time. I know this is not our fairy-tale ending, that we won't get to experience that life, but I kiss her so she knows without a doubt how I feel. When I'm hundreds of miles away it's her I'll be thinking about. I kiss her again so I can remember how kissing is supposed to feel in your toes, in your gut. I want to remember the fireworks her lips set off between my legs. She moans and I know she feels it too. A truck rumbles on the gravel a ways down the road and we jump apart. It's just a neighbor, Eileen explains as the man drives by. He waves and we wave back and then we head back toward home.

It's a long time before I write Eileen again. I didn't know what to say. That kiss broke something in me, for better or for worse. I can't look at Walter the same. Every intimate moment we have, it's thoughts of Eileen that help me finish. Everything in my life is a lie.

Her next letter is the one that changes everything. The paper is nearly falling apart, I've read it so many times. It's short, but it says everything I need to hear.

Dear Juney, I love you. I'm putting on a brave face for Harry and the kids, but I'm thinking of you all the time. I can't leave him. He's innocent in all this, and it feels wrong to just toss him aside because of feelings I can't control, and I have to think about the kids too, but I do love you. My heart is yours, Eileen

* * *

Eileen looks up from the pages.

"I wrote this while Cole was napping. Woke her up and we went right to the post office."

"This was the one you didn't want Harry to find," I say. In her next letter she begged me to burn it. I didn't.

"I didn't want Harry to find any of them. I'm glad you kept it."

After that we barely mention our husbands and our kids anymore. We talk about what we want, what we wish we had. I tell her, now that I'm paying closer attention, I know women who are living together. People think them widowed or sisters or even just strange, but they are making it work. Eileen understands, but she can't leave Harry. Still she writes. The letters become more frequent and more open. I keep them all.

Dear Juney, I had a dream about you last night. You were chasing me through the pines. The sun was out and it was raining. I let you catch me this time. Even though we can't be together, you are still in my heart. Forever yours, Eileen

We go five more years without seeing each other. Between her letters, I focus on the boys and my students. Slowly, I start to let Walter go. It starts with my classes, more students now that the boys are older. More Saturday afternoons apart and more evenings where I leave dinner for him in the fridge. Then I start coming to bed later and later. It's easier to deny a man who's already asleep. He asks me once if there's someone else. I don't even sound offended when I tell him no.

Later that week I meet a woman at the library. There's no attraction, but she tells me about a great dance workshop they're having at NYU. I hide my left hand the whole time and don't tell her I'm married. When I meet her by the ticket booth a few days later, my ring is zipped into my purse. I tell Eileen about her in my next letter. I'm happy to hear that she's jealous when she writes back.

There's a spring wedding. Eileen's oldest, Patricia, is pregnant, but that's between the families and the pages of our letters. Eileen invites us down. Walter agrees, thinking we'll find our romance somewhere in that Southern heat, but all I find is Eileen the morning of the ceremony. We're alone in the powder room at the church. She doesn't say a word, but her eyes tell me everything. She's been waiting for this one stolen moment for us. I seize it, not knowing if we'll ever get another. I kiss her, and this time it's aching and pain and relief. We've had time apart, time to think things through, but the feelings haven't changed. I love her and I know she loves me too.

"I don't know what to do," she whispers as my lips brush her forehead. I know what I want her to do, but mostly it's what I want for myself. I don't have it in me to ask Eileen to be that selfish.

"We endure it."

She stares back at me and I offer her what I can of a reassuring smile. She nods. I hold her a moment longer even though I know we are out of time. We both turn back to the mirror and fix our lipstick. The last time I dance with Walter is at that reception.

Six months later I move out. I tell Walter 90 percent of the truth: that I'm gay and that I can't be with him anymore. He doesn't understand, and neither do the boys. I'm the villain for a long time, but I know the decision is right. My confidence wavers, though, when I see that I've made this decision alone.

I'm free of Walter, but no closer to Eileen. It's a struggle not to beg in my letters to her. It takes everything I have to balance an expression of love and the bottomless desperation that claws at my heels.

Harry's heart attack surprises everyone, but I'm relieved by Eileen's first letter after his funeral. I don't think it's appropriate for me to attend.

Dear Juney, I don't know how to say this, but I will. I miss Harry. He was a good man. I already miss his companionship and I miss him for the kids, but I feel free. Is that horrible for me to say? I know it is, but I've always told you the truth. How much longer can you wait for me? Forever Yours, Eileen.

By now there are cell phones and we text each other pictures of our grandkids, but I need my reply documented correctly.

Forever, I write back.

It doesn't take forever, but it feels that way. Four more years. Two for the kids. A year for them to process that she is not what they thought her to be. And in that time, months to learn of her feelings for me, time for them to form an opinion on those feelings. Eileen's pre-diabetic and her doctor wants her to lose a few pounds. She says she wants to look good for me. There's another year, and then Eileen needs some time for herself. I tell her I can wait. She calls me late one night.

"We should take a trip first. I want to go to Las Vegas and Paris. You can show me all the fancy French you learned."

I think of the money Walter was kind enough to tell me to save, and Eileen tells me she has plenty from Harry.

"We'll take a trip, then." I feel myself smiling in the dark.

"What do we do after the trip?"

"I figure if I can handle traveling with you, I can handle living with you."

"You want to move to New York?"

"You keep saying the city keeps you young."

"That's true, but—"

"Then I'll come live with you. After our trip. Night." She hangs up before I can argue. Later, though, I give her a practical out. If the trip is too overwhelming, she can go back to Mississippi with no fight from me. With all this time gone by, I need her to be happy.

She's near now and I can't read the expression on her face.

"Will you touch me?" she asks. I get up and scoot into the booth beside her. Under the table I take her hand. Everything feels right. For a moment.

"I thought it would be easier. I thought I would feel...lighter. Freer?" she says.

"But you don't."

"I don't know how you made it through. I never thought I could be so lonely."

I hold my breath and think things through before I react. She's sad. She's hurting, but she's here. That matters.

"What do we do?"

"We travel. Like we planned," she says.

"I want you to be sure."

"I am."

"Then we'll decide when we get back."

"I said, I am." She shakes her head and tries again. "I'm saying this all wrong. I think I feel guilty. About Harry and the kids. I feel bad because I feel so good about being here with you. I've wanted to be here with you all along."

"You know what I've realized," I say. "It's okay to feel two ways about things. It's okay that you care about your family and their needs. I never wanted that to stop."

"I know."

I turn and look at Eileen. For once it's not a secret. We don't have to hide. I kiss her. She kisses me back. We keep it tame because we're in public and there's no need to frighten the young people. Later, things will get more interesting.

She sighs and puts her head on my shoulder. We're nine again, hiding under the church porch. Eileen yawns and tells me her grandma lost another tooth. I laugh to myself and tell Eileen why. She laughs too and squeezes my hand back.

I kiss her again, and this time we have an audience.

"Ow, ow! Get it, Grandma." Two teenagers at the counter are watching us. The yeller winks. Her friend gives us a thumbs-up and a toothy grin. Beside me, Eileen laughs and I feel it down in my gut. She's happy. She's relieved. And so am I.

A STORY ABOUT SARAH

Cheyenne Blue

They tell you that when you start writing things down, you should write about what you know and what you love. When my head was so full of stories that I had to let some loose, I started with those that were easiest to tell.

What do I know: I know how to sing. I know how to cook. I know how the land smells after the rain that rarely falls. I know how to stop a child's tears although I've no kids of my own. I know how to gentle a skittish colt so that he follows me around like a dog. And I know Sarah.

What do I love: I love this land, I love its silence and its emptiness. I love the red rocks that jumble along the creek. I love the gargle of magpies in the morning. I love how under my hands food comes together to make a meal. And I love Sarah.

This, then, is a story about Sarah. It's the first story that fell out of my head, but stories about Sarah are as many and winding as the tracks on a scribbly gum.

My name is Melly and I'm forty-four years old. I'm half

Yamatji and half white. The Yamatji half came from the desert in Western Australia, where I sometimes go; the white half came from Germany, where I've never been. My Yamatji mother died when I was little, or maybe she went outback. I like to think of her roaming the land, digging for grubs, knowing where to find food, living the old way. Maybe she died of drink, but I don't want to know if she did.

I cook for the workers here at the mining camp where I live. I got the job when I was fifteen. My German pa worked at the camp, and we lived here as well. Most of the kids wanted to leave. They wanted to go to Perth or to the shore where the waves curled. Not me. I wanted to stay in this sunburned little settlement. So I took the first job that was offered.

I met Sarah when I was sixteen and she was a year older. She also worked at the camp, in the office. Her pa was the mine manager, and Sarah used to do something with books and paper. We were the only two girls there, so it was natural that we'd hang together. Sarah never minded the color of my skin. It mattered to people then. It doesn't now.

Sarah was slender, back when we were girls. She was skinny, with knees that were the widest part of her legs, and a chest like a boy's. She had long curly brown hair that fell nearly to her waist. She wore it in a thick plait down her back, all crinkly and barely contained. Now she's sturdy and wide, and she has breasts that are ample and spreading. Her hair is still thick and curly, but now there's gray in it, and it's short and hugs her head. That's Sarah.

The boys at the mine all wanted to take Sarah out, but her pa kept a strict eye on her. The boys didn't want to take me out, at least not where we would be seen. And I didn't want to go with them anyway. Instead, Sarah and I would go places together: down to the billabong to swim, up the wallaby path to the top of the rocks where we'd sit and look out over the camp. Sometimes we'd spy on the men and giggle. More often, we'd sit in the shade of a scribbly gum and talk.

This is a story about Sarah, but it's also a story about Sarah and me. Sarah and me together. She kissed me the first time. I kissed her back the second time. The times after that, I don't remember. We weren't girls then. I was twenty, she a year older. And then we were lovers.

We'd do our loving outdoors, always in the open, never in my room at the camp or at her da's house. We'd climb to the top of the rocks where there was a hidden place. The red sand was soft, and there was patchy shade when the sun was low. Best of all, you'd never guess it was there, not unless you happened over the rocks, not following any path, and stumbled across it. So we never worried about being caught. I'm not sure what would have happened had someone found us, but it doesn't matter now. After nearly thirty years together, most of them know and most of them don't care. Any that do care stay away.

We had a blanket that we stashed in a cranny in the rocks. We'd shake it out well, so that the spiders and sometimes a scorpion or little tiger snake were dislodged, and we'd spread it down on the sand. We'd take off our clothes immediately. There was no delicate disrobing, we'd just stand and undress. The red sand would spill over the edge of the blanket and often our skin would be so wet with sweat that the sand would stick, coating us with marbled patterns of red. It seemed right to be naked there, out in the sun, out on the earth. Once we were undressed, we'd never put our clothes back on until it was time to walk home. Have you ever been naked under the sun? If you have, you'll never forget it.

Sometimes we still do our loving outdoors, although it's not as easy for us to climb the rocks to reach our place, and often we're too lazy.

This is a story about Sarah and how she kisses.

At first, we did nothing but kiss. Gentle kisses, almost chaste. Sarah says that she wanted to make them into more, but she was afraid of what I'd do, what I'd say, how I'd laugh at her. But I wanted the same, and one day, suddenly, we were really kissing. Tongues together, and there were wet lips and saliva and it was all very hot and desperate. I loved her kisses. I loved how her lips were so firm and how soft they would be if it weren't for the sand that coated them. There was an edge of pain from the way that the grains rubbed and ground into our lips. She'd stop and wipe the sand from my lips and hers with a finger, but it was no good. It would be back again the next time.

It was a long time before we did anything but kiss. Months. Why seek more when what you have is so perfect? Sarah's kisses are like the creek that flows down the red bluff after rain: at first it's barely there, the merest hint of what's to come, before it swells and falls into something so deep you could drown in it. Then it overflows, and unleashed it swirls into a fierce, raging passion.

This is a story about Sarah and how she likes to be loved.

Sarah likes to be in charge. When we make love, she likes to direct how it will go. She leads my fingers to where she wants them on her body. I never mind, as I love her skin and I love to caress her, slowly if that's what she wants, so slowly that I think I can feel each pore, each grain of sand on her skin. I love to touch her breasts like that, circling around and around, a sort of aimless pattern that is not actually aimless at all, closer and closer to her nipple. Sarah's breasts were tiny and barely there once. Now they're ripe and full and lush, just as she is. When I stroke her like this, she wiggles like a black snake caught by the tail, twisting, trying to slide her body under my fingers if they won't move faster over her body.

"Mel-ly," she says, and my name is broken down into long pieces, each a part of the whole. Sometimes she just calls me Mel, and when she does, I think she's leaving part of me behind.

When my fingers finally find her nipple, she sighs, just once, as if she's come home. Maybe she has. Her nipples are sensitive and she doesn't like them treated roughly. So I worship them, stroking their dark peaks, as dark and red as desert flowers, and then take one of them in my mouth and suck gently, oh so gently. She loves that, and her hands wind into my hair, not holding me there, just letting me know she likes what I'm doing.

Sarah lets me know when she wants more. If I touch her cunt before she wants it, she'll push my hand away, gently, not rudely, just telling me she's not quite ready. I stroke her waist while I'm waiting for her signal, the indent above her hips—once so narrow and boyish, now wider with padding that hides her bones. I kiss her tummy, tickling with my tongue to make her giggle or sigh, and I stroke her thighs, feeling for that special place on the inside where the skin is softest.

I can always smell her cunt. Sarah's smell is different from mine—and I have no one else to compare with. She smells musky and warm like fresh baked bread, salty like the sea, sharp like bush lemons. When she's excited, her woman-smell surrounds her so that I can taste it on her skin, not only in her pussy.

When she wants me to touch her cunt, she takes my hand and pushes it down. Or she'll shift so that she's sitting and open her legs invitingly. I'll use my fingers to stroke, to circle her clit with the light touch she loves—too heavy and she'll flinch away. I'll push two, three fingers up inside her and I'll use my thumb to rub. My hands are as dexterous as a piano player's. She hums and I play.

I taste her. I eat her. I push my face up between her legs so far that my nose is wedged against her mound, my chin wet with her juices. She smells so strong then, and I love it. I lick her delicately, using my tongue all around her pussy, pushing it inside, and then around and around her clit. She's vocal, my Sarah, and she hums and sighs and grunts in pleasure. Sometimes she'll hold my head, trying to direct me, but I've been doing this for so long that I know the moves, I know the paths that she loves the most.

She shivers when she comes, a whole-body sort of shiver that starts at her toes, travels up along her legs, so tautly held, and into her rigid abdomen. She clenches down, as if pushing herself into the blanket, into the red earth, will make her come harder. If my fingers are inside her, I can feel her internal little tremors too, all flicker and shivery. It would be a delicate dance around my fingers, except that she's so strong. She always comes. Once, maybe twice.

This is a story about Sarah, and how she loves.

Sarah likes to surprise, which is the opposite of how she likes me to love her. Sometimes she blindfolds me and leaves me lying there in the patterns of sunlight. I can barely breathe when she does that. I lie there waiting for her to touch me, wondering where it will be. Maybe she'll kiss me again, maybe she'll kiss my breast, or my belly, or the rise of my hipbone. Maybe she'll just spread my thighs and plunge her tongue into my cunt. Or maybe she'll brush me with scratchy piece of bark, or trickle hot sand onto my skin from a height, so that the grains pepper me like buckshot, before forming their own little pyramid. Sometimes an insect will run over my skin and I won't know if it's her. That makes her laugh in delight.

Always, though, Sarah likes to please.

"D'you like that?" she says, or "That feel good?" Even when

she knows the answer—which is most of the time after all our time together—she still likes to ask. And she catalogs my grunts and sighs and incoherent responses and works out the answer for herself.

Sarah likes to use her fingers more than her tongue, as then she can watch my face. She says I'm most beautiful when I come. I don't believe her, but I like to hear her say it anyway. So most of the time, she uses her fingers—three, four, sometimes her whole hand—and she pistons and thrusts and fucks me as hard as I can take. Her fingers are nimble and flexible. She knows my insides better than I do, and she knows where to press so that I come alive under her hand. She can make me wetter than the creek in no time at all, and the wetter I get, the more she likes it.

Afterward, when I've come so hard that my stomach muscles ache with the spasms, she cradles my head and strokes my hair from my face and croons to me.

This is a story about Sarah, and me and her together.

It's not just about her. It's not just me doing her, and it's not just about me either. It's give and take. We both know what we like, and we share that giving. We know which one of us needs it first, needs it most. And afterward, we lie together on the bright blanket with the gray-green leaves overhead. The air is hot and dry, and our skin is hot and damp. Afterward, it's about patterns. The leaves above our heads, the movement of her breath on my skin, the ritual of our loving completed. If I close my eyes, the sun and shade are still there behind my eyelids, and Sarah is there too. She's always there, in my head.

We get up and take turns brushing the sand from our bodies. Then we dress, putting on shorts and T-shirts, and we roll up the blanket and put it back in the nook in the rocks for the next time. Hand in hand, we wander back to our weatherboard house at the edge of the camp that we've shared for the last twenty-one years. It has a verandah that looks west, toward the ocean, although the ocean is far, far away. Sarah and I sit on our big double rocker, drink a cold beer and watch the sunset. Sarah thinks of the ocean, and how she'd like to feel the salt water surround her.

I think of Sarah, and how I'd like to feel her surround me again.

This was a story about Sarah. Sarah and me. Together.

WAITING FOR THE HARVEST

Sommer Marsden

Seriously. How long?" I hissed this right into Misty's ear and saw her grin in the orange Halloween glow of the campfire.

"Calm down, baby," she said through rigid teeth. Her mouth did not move, and her words came out stilted. The grin never left her handsome face.

"Calm down? These people think they can control the weather!" I breathed. It was one thing to come at Misty's acupuncturist's invitation. It was another thing to listen to the attendees wax poetic about being weather workers.

I was all for diversity, but the whole thing was creeping me out a bit.

Misty leaned into me, snaking one long arm around my shoulder, and said in my ear—so my shoulders shook with a shiver and my nipples peaked under my thin pink tee—"Listen up, Meredith. We are going to sit here for a few. Then we are going to go peruse Bruce's organic veggies that he's invited everyone to take home with them. Then you are going to plead a headache, and we are going to beat feet like our asses are on fire before anyone can offer to stick needles in you to alleviate your pain. *Capisce?*"

Her voice was as smoky as the cool night air, and in the fire pit a sappy knot in the wood popped with a vengeance. I turned and kissed her right on her naked lips, which always somehow tasted of strawberries. "I have never been more turned on by you," I admitted.

"You know it," she said and smiled. I sat in my lawn chair watching orange bits of fire float up to the heavens until she squeezed my hand, signaling our nonchalant mosey over to the vegetable table the host had set up.

Bruce had informed everyone of his abundant organic garden harvest upon arrival. We'd all been invited to take baskets of veggies home with us. I couldn't help but mentally roll my eyes when he'd said, "All of this bounty has been tended to by my own loving hands. No pesticides or chemicals or falsities of any kind."

But I had to admit, they were gorgeous. "Tomatoes?" Misty asked.

"Yes," I said.

"Eggplant?" Misty hefted a huge aubergine eggplant and turned it in her hands. She stroked it almost sensually, and I felt my skin prickle with arousal.

"Yes," I said, a small catch in my voice.

She heard it and grinned at me. The firelight in the navy blue night made her teeth look big and white. The Cheshire Cat sprang to mind.

We moved down the table laden with bins of fresh-picked produce. "Beets?" She picked up two round root vegetables, their leafy tops swinging like a burlesque dancer's tassels.

"Yep. I love beets!"

"Parsnips?"

"I'd rather die," I said, my words a reminder to her of her infamous venison and parsnip stew that had found me charging from the room intent on brushing my teeth. For a year.

Misty reached into a blue bin and pulled out a handful of carrots. The green leafy whips of their tops draped over her hand. "Carrots?"

"Tons," I said. Carrots were my favorites. Raw, roasted, stewed, Crock-Potted within an inch of their thin orange lives. I loved carrots. I took one from her hand and stared. "Wow."

"What?" Misty pressed against me, peering at the vegetable in my hand.

"It is rather...male, isn't it?"

"Looks like a cock," Misty said.

I clapped my hands shut over the carrot and said, "Shh!"

"Is it a secret cock?"

I bit my lip to keep from laughing. "It reminds me of that cartoon you showed me that one time."

"The farmer's wife fucking herself with a carrot?"

"Yeah, that one." I opened my hands again and stared at the bulbous, phallic carrot.

Misty grabbed my hand and said into my ear, "Come on. Let's take your boyfriend home and put him to good use."

"What? What does that mean?" I squealed, but in my belly a warm stripe of anticipation flared hot. My skin pebbled all over and my scalp tingled with excitement.

"Come on. Stop bellyaching."

Misty said a speedy good-bye. Good-bye to the Reiki masters and acupuncturists. Good-bye to the psychics, the mediums and the weather workers.

"They know we're lying," I said as she hustled me to the car, the distant glow of the fire nothing more than an orange ball of intense light from this distance.

"So they'll strike us with lightning. It's a risk I'll take to fuck you," she said and slipped into the car. I had no choice but to follow.

"Wash this well. I'll be right back," Misty said. The way she said it sent a thrill up my spine. It was her no-nonsense, "you're about to be fucked, like it or not," voice, and after a night full of characters who leaned toward a bit of spiritual lunacy, I was ready for down-to-earth fucking.

I scrubbed the carrot and really looked it over. Its bushy green top was slick with water, and the top was as big around as three of my fingers bunched together. As long from tip to top as my middle finger to the bottom of my palm, it really was nature's dildo. Which made me snicker. I waved it at myself in the mirror and waggled my eyebrows. "Shall we leave the greens on, Mama?" I asked my reflection.

"Yes, let's," Misty said from the doorway, and I jumped.

"Oh, no," I said. For ages I had vetoed the long, thin, screaming orange strap-on. And now Misty stood there wearing it.

"Can you guess tonight's theme?" Misty asked, pulling my arm so I stumble-stepped from our tiny one-ass bathroom.

"Surreality?" I quipped

"Orange. Now come on then, Farmer Meredith. Let's get you out of these clothes so you can commune with nature."

I put my hand on her long, orange faux cock and said, "There's nothing natural about that." But my pussy went wet and soft and eager when I touched the long silicone appendage. I would never ever admit to it in a million years.

"No, but it sure as hell will be fun."

Misty had braided her dark red hair into long, thick braids. They hung down the sides and made her look like a cowgirl.

A cowgirl strapped and ready for action. That made me laugh again, but it was a high wild laugh that indicated nerves.

"Oh, but..." I eyed the carrot I clutched in a death grip and the fake cock jutting from her trim pelvis, and my cheeks burned like hothouse tomatoes in the sun. I was scared.

"Come on, city girl. Let the farmer show you how we do it in the sticks." She rubbed her strap-on against my leg and chuckled softly. It was that sexy, self-assured chuckle that did me in.

"Okay," I whispered.

Misty led me to our room and bumped me with her hips so I hit the bed with my ass first. She tugged my jeans and panties down after wrestling my boots free of my feet. Her fingers tripped each pearlescent button on my blue button-down, and she freed me of my bra. When I was naked, she took my bare foot and kissed my toes, finally kissing her way up my inner legs until I was vibrating with a fine tremor of want.

"I'll make it good for you, city girl," she said, kissing the crease where my thigh met my pussy. She pressed the pads of her cool fingers just outside my nether lips and pressed, sending a pleasant pressure through my cunt. Then she speared me with her wet, hot tongue, putting me out of my anticipatory misery. "I'll make you so wet you'll be begging for it," she said.

When she sucked my clit in alternating rhythms, I believed her. "I never beg," I said, but my voice was so watery no one—including me—believed me at all.

"Okay," she said, laughing softly. The vibration of her amusement skittered up my inner thigh to my belly. Misty pushed a finger into me, thrust and moved and pressed and then took it out. I gasped.

"Hey!"

"Shh," she said and put her lips back to my pussy. Wet circles and patterns and flat, broad licks of her tongue, and I was dancing on my back. Then a finger and a twist and a press and all my nerve endings sang out with joy and then—she'd withdraw.

"Oh, my god," I said.

"Shh." Licking and sucking and flicking. More sucking. More fingers, and she found my G-spot and I shuddered. And then her fingers were gone.

"Okay! Okay! Do me now! Spear me with your pickle!" I snorted, breaking the sex-soaked spell, but only for a moment.

"It's a carrot. Well, a pseudo carrot," she said, but she flipped me on my belly and patted my ass. "Hands and knees, baby. Like a horse." Then it was her turn to snort, and I heard the distinctive sound of the lube bottle.

Her fingers pressed deep into my ass. Drenched in lube, she slid right in on a moan from me. "Nice," Misty breathed. "You really do want my pickle."

"Carrot," I reminded her in a soft voice.

"Right. Speaking of...got yours?"

I reached out to find our prized organic carrot and waved it so the ends rustled like pom-poms.

"Good girl." Then she positioned the tip of her glowing orange cock to my ass and pushed. A steady pressure that built until I was breathing out a long breath through that pinchy pain that always came, and god, she was in, and I was so full. Misty froze and reached her hand out, her voice drunk with lust now that she was in and that nub in her harness was rubbing her clit. "Give it to me."

I handed her the carrot, only able to focus on the intense pleasurable pressure in my ass and the fact that my clit seemed to be beating in time with my heart. "Hurry," I said. My cunt flexed and spasmed around nothing, my nerve endings all alive at once as my body flirted with the swiftly approaching orgasm.

"Shh," she said, again. It seemed to be her theme word for the night.

Misty started to move, and I forgot about people clustered around a fire, discussing controlling the elements. I forgot that I was afraid of the orange-strap on. I almost forgot she was about to fuck me with a vegetable. Until she pushed the scrubbed-clean, warm-from-the-tap-water carrot to my slippery pussy and thrust.

And then I truly was full. So full of her cock and the lusty vegetable all I could do was hang my head and rock back against her. It wasn't a long time coming, that first orgasm. It rocketed toward me with frightening speed as she drove into my ass, working my pussy with our freshly harvested phallus.

"Oh, god," I said.

"Farmer," she said. There was humor in her tone, but more than anything, there was arousal. Her voice was husky with it. Her warm nipples rubbed my back as she covered me, pressed to me, pressed into me. Fucked me completely.

"Farmer," I said, "I love your carrot."

I sighed. The orgasm took me under, and I pressed my forehead to the cool blue wall above our bed. Misty thrust harder into my ass, her own pleasure building, I could tell by her breath.

"Carrots," she said, exaggerating the *S* and thrusting into my spasming pussy with her root vegetable. The green top hissed and rustled under me, and I wondered, wildly, if we'd be picking greens out of our bed for weeks.

"I'm going to come soon," she said, rotating her hips in that way she always did when trying to ward off an orgasm that was coming too fast for her. Like she could fend it off with flicks of her trim hips.

"Good," I said, snorting. I meant it. I loved to hear her come.

The only thing better than hearing it was seeing it. But my head was pressed to the wall, and my girlfriend was pressed to my ass.

"No, no," she said, stilling her body but fucking me more briskly with that randy carrot. "I know you have one more in you. I can feel it. Give. It. To. Me."

She moved just a bit. Just enough that I felt her fullness warring with the carrot's fullness in my cunt, and then she bent to nip me on my side. Right above the ladder of my ribs. Her small white teeth found me, and she was moving, working her voodoo sex magic as usual.

I came with an "Oh, Farmer!"

And Misty started to grind into me, her hips banging, her breath rushed. She came with a long, low sigh, her fingers digging into my skin hard enough to bruise. And then she said, "Now, for *that*, I'd get up and till the fields any day."

"Not me," I said, pressing my forehead to our cool sheets, waiting for my heart to calm. "If you don't mind, I'll be in bed waiting for the harvest."

SEPIA SHOWERS

Andrea Dale

I don't usually bring Kathy with me when I visit my mother.

Oh, my mother knows that Kathy's my friend, that we share a house. But I don't know if, when she was more lucid or now, my mother ever figured out that Kathy and I were *together.*

Now, it doesn't seem worth it to try and explain. While my mother hasn't (yet) forgotten who I am, other people in her periphery have become more fluid. And although I've never exactly hidden my preferences, I don't think my mother ever fully comprehended that I'm a lesbian.

My father, god rest his soul, would never have understood. It became second nature to me not to spill the truth.

"It's time for me to go, Mom," I say. It's past time, really, but it's always hard for me to leave. I know how alone she must feel, despite the staff who check in on her several times a day, make sure she takes her pills and eats balanced meals.

It's dementia, but a mild form. She remembers me, knows the people around her. It's the day-to-day things she forgets.

Where she put things. Whether she ate. Where my father, who died last year, has gotten to this time.

I know it could be far worse, but it's still hard.

I start to rise, but she doesn't let go of my hand. "I just wish you'd find someone, Dana," she says. "A good man to make you happy."

I smile for her. "I'll see what I can do."

But before I can get up, she looks over my shoulder. Her eyes widen and her free hand goes to her throat in shock. "Charlotte?" she whispers.

I turn. "Oh, Mom, it's just Kathy, here to pick me up. You remember Kathy, don't you?"

Kathy steps into the room. "Hi, Mrs. Hollander."

"Oh, Kathy, of course. Pardon my manners." My mom reaches out to take Kathy's hand. "You just reminded me of someone for a moment there."

We say our good-byes, and I gather up the box of photos she's sending home with me. In the doorway, I glance back. Mom's looking at the picture of my father on the table next to her chair.

I wish, more than anything, I could tell her that I *have* found someone, someone who makes me deliriously happy.

But I can't.

When we get home, Kathy makes tea. Lady Grey, my favorite. She knows I need to wind down. I wrap my hands around the cup as she drapes the hand-woven mohair blanket over our laps. A watery slate blue, it's the first thing we bought when we moved in together, and now it smells like roses because she'd been sitting against it earlier today.

We burrow into each other and the sofa.

I sigh, just shy of contentment. "My poor mom."

"Oh?"

She's stroking my hair. I should be too old to enjoy such a simple act.

"She wants me to find a nice man who'll make me happy."

We both laugh at the irony of that. It feels good to let the sound bubble out of me, releasing the tension in my chest, an ache I didn't even realize was there until now.

"I'm sorry," I say to Kathy now. "I don't like keeping you a secret. I'm not ashamed of us, you know..."

"Oh, dear heart, I know. I've always known. And it's okay. I don't want to cause your mom distress any more than you do."

Her parents know about us, embrace us and adore me so much that Kathy jokes if we split up, they'll keep me instead of her.

"The more important question," she continues, "is what's in the box?"

"Pictures," I say. "Uncle Dan's been reorganizing the storage unit and brought them to her, and she thought I'd like to go through them. I'll scan them, and hopefully get some stories out of her before..."

I can't say the words "before it's too late," but Kathy knows. She kisses my head, my cheek, and I take a few shuddery breaths to center myself.

Later that night, when I most want to sleep, most want to run away from the thoughts, I lie awake. When Kathy rolls over and spoons against me, her back to my front, I snake my hand beneath her arm and grope for her hand. In her sleep, she twines her fingers with mine.

It's all I can do not to squeeze so hard I wake her.

How can it be possible to forget?

I don't want to forget.

I press my face into her shoulder. The soft strands of her hair tickle my face. Disengaging my hand, I gently run it across her hip, savoring the spot at the joint that's warmer than the rest of her, then down her thigh. She's taken up running again in an effort to stave off the middle-age spread, and even with my light touch, I can feel the muscles, hard and strong.

I hadn't been thinking about sex, really, I hadn't, but apparently my exploring hand plants the idea in Kathy's subconscious. Still asleep, she murmurs, a happy hum of a sound, and presses herself back against me.

I vow never to forget the feeling of her body against mine, nor how my body responds to it. My nipples harden, pressing against her smooth back. Even in the dark, I know the constellation of freckles on her shoulders, and I trace them with my lips and tongue, still gentle, easing her into wakefulness. At the same time, I snake my hand back up to circle her nipples with my fingertips, feeling them crinkle in response.

When she does finally rouse, she's already half-aroused: I can smell her earthy musk. I move my hand to touch her, but she captures my wrist.

"No," she whispers. "Let me."

I assume she means she'll pleasure herself—although, half-lust-fogged myself, I'm not sure why—but instead she rolls over, insinuating one of those strong thighs between mine, pressing against my mound. Almost involuntarily, I grind against her, smearing her skin with my own wetness.

I hadn't realized how excited I'd become, either.

She cups my face, then tangles her fingers in my hair, pulling me in for a kiss that starts sweet but rapidly grows urgent. Now I feel almost frantic, not for orgasm, but to kiss her, feel her lips and teeth and tongue; to lose myself in the sensation and forget my sadness.

But not forget her, not forget how she feels, how she makes me feel. Never that.

She rolls me on my back, rises above me, her thigh flexing against me as she takes first one, then the other nipple in her mouth. We're past the soft strokes like the ones I used to wake her; now she's nipping, pinching, tweaking.

I'm ramping up, passion overtaking rational thought, and yet the two are fighting against each other. I want to track every sensation—her flesh against mine, her quick breaths, the taste of that drop of sweat I just kissed off her forehead—create snapshot memories, preserve them.

But then she begs, "Come on, baby. Come for me." Her voice is tight, and I know she's on the verge, too, from the way I've been humping up against her in my own quest for orgasm.

"You...first..."

"No." It's a moan. "You."

I'm not sure which one of us starts first, just that one triggers the other, and back again, and again. We build on each other's joy, a twining spiral of fever pitch and release.

"I love you," she whispers, and I'm sure I will always remember that sound, and the catch in my own throat as I say it back to her.

Now, exhausted, I finally sleep.

I'm busy the next few days, so it's a while before I have the chance to look through the box of photos. I curl up on the sofa with another cup of tea. Kathy's already there, feet propped up, laptop keys clicking as she works.

She puts down the computer and sets her glasses on her nose. They're from the dollar store, shocking green, and she wears them on a beaded chain she made. I don't need reading glasses—yet—but I borrow them a couple of times to look at some of the older photos where the faces are small and a little blurred.

Then I pull out one, and in my own intake of breath I can hear the echo of my mother's gasp from the other day, when she saw Kathy.

Kathy plucks the photo out of my hand. Her eyes widen.

"Yeah," I say. "So, are you a vampire or a time-traveling alien?"

The picture is of my mom, I'm guessing during college from her age and clothes. The black-and-white photo shows her with another young woman, their arms around each other's waists as they laugh into the camera. My mom's scarf is whipping in the wind, while the other woman has a hand up to keep her own hat from blowing away.

The other woman, who looks a hell of a lot like Kathy.

Kathy flips the picture over. "Betsy and Charlotte," she deciphers the faded penciled words. "Who was Charlotte?"

"I have no idea." I dig into the box. "I don't remember Mom ever mentioning her."

There are more photos of Charlotte, more than I've seen of any other friends of my mom from that era. The ones she'd been close to, she was still in contact with (if they were still alive)...or so I'd thought. The more we find, the more we realize Kathy isn't Charlotte's doppelgänger, but at the right angles, there's certainly a resemblance.

And, I suspect, there had been something going on between my mother and the lovely Charlotte.

"Tell me if I'm losing my mind..." I begin.

"Always," Kathy vows. I smack her thigh, which reminds me of a few nights ago, which distracts me for a moment.

"There's something about the way Charlotte is looking at the camera in some of these," I finally say. "And the way my mom and Charlotte are together. I know women were...they held hands as friends more often then, that sort of thing. But I feel like I'm seeing a...closer relationship?"

"I was actually thinking the same thing," Kathy agrees. "These shots here, of the two of them"— she fans them out on the coffee table—"I think they might have been done with a self-timer, rather than someone else taking the picture."

"Which might explain why they were free to be so... snuggly."

"I think," Kathy says with a grin, "that your mother might have some 'splaining to do."

By the time I visit my mother the next day after work, I've convinced myself I've been reading too much into the pictures.

We have our usual hellos, the small talk about the food at the home, that she won at bingo yesterday. Then I bring out the manila envelope.

"I started scanning those pictures you gave me," I say. She doesn't remember, so I remind her about Uncle Dan bringing them. I'm not sure if she agrees because I jog her memory or because she doesn't want to admit she's forgotten—whether to me or herself isn't clear. Is that what we fall into? Playing games with ourselves, convincing ourselves everything is okay?

"I was wondering," I continue, handing her a photo. "Who's Charlotte? I don't think you've ever mentioned her before."

I watch as an array of emotions cross my mother's face. I'm not imagining things. I see fondness, sadness...love.

"She was a friend," my mom says.

"From the looks of it, she was more than a friend," I say.

She glances at me. I raise my eyebrows, but I also smile. "Mom," I say gently. "You can tell me."

She bites her lip, and tears fill her eyes. She doesn't cry, though—she's cried in front of me only once before, and that was when my father died. Our family, we don't believe in that sort of thing. Thankfully Kathy's broken me of that bad habit.

And then my mother tells me the story. Not in graphic terms; in fact, she dances and skirts around things, darting looks at me to see if I'm picking up the innuendo. Then she looks away again, lost in a memory that thankfully she still has, still clings to.

What comes out is roughly what I'd suspected: A college fling, she says, that nobody else knew about. It was more than that, though: I can tell from her voice that she'd loved Charlotte. She tells me she and Charlotte had a relationship, but it wasn't as accepted back then, and—as she insists over and over—she loved my father very much. I'm tempted to say, "So you're bisexual—that's fantastic," but I think using the word will shut her down.

So I give her my support, my understanding. She seems to relax when she realizes I'm not judging or questioning her.

Ever since I saw the photos of her and Charlotte and guessed what might have happened, I'd been thinking. My mother may have dementia, but she hasn't forgotten everything. I can't treat her like a child.

She wants me to be happy. She deserves to know I am.

I tell her about Kathy.

My mother is silent for a long while. A heavy knot forms in my stomach. Was this a mistake?

Then, finally, she asks, "Are you happy?"

"Happier than I ever could have imagined," I tell her. "She's the one, Mom. I'm going to spend the rest of my life with her."

"It won't be easy," she says. She always has to warn me of the negative side of things.

"We've been together for eleven years," I say. "We've weathered the negative so far."

"Well, then," my mother says. "Well. What I want to know is, when's the wedding? When do I get to walk you down the aisle?"

I laugh, and we cry, and then we talk about wedding dresses.

We have the ceremony in the courtyard of the care facility. Just family and a few close friends. The water splashing in the fountain sparkles in the sunlight, and the color in the tiles are mirrored in the riotously blooming flowers.

On our wedding night, kissing Kathy is like kissing her for the first time and the millionth time, new and yet familiar, fresh and yet filled with the memories of every kiss we've shared.

Before I fall into the mindless spiral of desire, though, I realize something.

What's important isn't the future, isn't the possible forgetting. What's important is right now, this moment, glorying in everything that it is with no other goal than mutual pleasure.

Someday, down the line, we might forget the person...but we can never forget the love.

PALABRAS

Anna Meadows

The only secret I ever kept from Sawyer fit inside an orange crate.

She almost found it once, the day we moved in together. I had buried it in the backseat of my car, beneath my great-aunt's quilts and the box that held my mixing bowls. When I saw Sawyer come up the stairs with that wooden crate my grandfather had painted the cobalt of a blue glass jar, my heart was tight as a knot in cherry wood.

I told her that the things inside had belonged to my grandfather, that I kept them only because they smelled like him, like the cardamom of his favorite *tortas* and the loose tobacco he rolled into paper. They would mean nothing to me if it weren't for that, I told her. It could have been anything, I said, as long as it held that same spice and earth.

She believed me. They always believe you if you want it enough.

And it wasn't all a lie. Everything in that crate my grandfather gave me, and every time I took it down from the top of the closet, the whole apartment smelled like my grandmother's *pan de muerto*. That's why I never took it down unless I knew there was enough time to let that perfume slip out the open windows before Sawyer got home. The few times I spent so long fingering its contents that the scent was too heavy to dissipate, I made *tortas de aceite* with enough cardamom that Sawyer didn't notice.

Sometimes I longed to show her everything in that orange crate, to spill its contents onto our bed and give over its secrets. But I didn't want to lose her. "Never let the boy think you are smarter than he is, *m'ija*," my mother told me. "You never keep him if he thinks you're smart." When I met Sawyer, I thought the same went for a woman who dressed like a boy.

My mother hated that my grandfather gave me so many books. He told me I was smart and that if I did not read enough, I would get lonely. "You want to know things," he said. He could tell by the ring of blue-black around the brown of my irises. So he brought me a book each time he came to visit. One month a book of Irish poets who sang of a land so green it broke their hearts open. Another, a dictionary, because whenever I asked my mother what a word meant she said, "You ask so many questions, you stop being pretty one day," and told me to stir the Spanish rice. For my birthday, a hardcover about the birds of the cloud forests where he met my grandmother. Its glossy pages shined with the emerald of hummingbirds and the blue tourmaline of the *quetzal*'s tail feathers.

He had brought me books for two years when my mother told me I was getting too smart. "No boy likes you if you talk like that," she said. *"Todas aquellas palabras."* All those words. It was two months before my thirteenth birthday, and she bleached my hair to the yellow of the *masa* we used for tamales. She said making me blonde would make up for all those books because my hair would keep boys from seeing those rings of midnight blue around my eyes.

Even after my grandfather was gone, my mother kept dyeing my hair. When I moved out, I did it myself, a force of habit as strong as biting my nails or reading *la Biblia* before bed. I knew she was right. I needed the maize-gold of my hair to hide what my grandfather had seen. He might have loved me for it, but no boy would.

When I moved in with Sawyer, I had to get rid of most of my grandfather's books. I could only keep as many as I could hide. Choosing which would stay was harder than picking which doll and which two dresses to take with me when I was a little girl and my family had to evacuate for the canyon fires. It was harder than how I never opened my eyes all the way in front of Sawyer, afraid she'd see those rings of blue. She always thought it was how I flirted with her, half closing my eyes like that.

A book about chaos theory had taught me that a butterfly flitting its wings at just the right time off the coast of my *abuela*'s hometown in Guatemala could turn the tide of the Mediterranean Sea. It sounded so much like a fairy tale, that little winged creature pulling on the oceans as much as the moon, that I grew drunk off dreams of *las mariposas* and a million coins of water. It had to come with me.

A small paperback, a French children's book about a boy who loved a rose so much it lit all the stars for him, more than earned the sliver of space it took up in the orange crate. The corners of a picture guide to the wildflowers of North America were still soft from my grandfather's thumbs, so I kept it. I held on to a hardcover of Neruda's poems if only for the line, "I do not love you as if you were salt-rose or topaz."

Books would not have been such a secret for most women.

They would have slid them onto the same shelves with their lovers', letting the spines mix until they could not have remembered whose began as whose if not for the names written onto the flyleaves. But I never forgot my mother telling me, "Never let the boy think you are smart." Sawyer loved me for my push-up bras and rosewater perfume, my cayenne-colored lipstick and all that yellow hair I made endless with hot rollers each morning. It didn't matter that by the time we'd been together for three years, she knew I dyed it.

I loved Sawyer for her saffron-colored hair, always just long enough to get in her eyes. I loved her for how the weight of the Leatherman on her belt pulled her jeans just enough to show a band of bare skin at the small of her back. I loved that her tongue always tasted like salt water.

I loved these things about her the way she loved those things about me, so it was not fair to let her know I was curious and smart like my grandfather had told me. It would have changed too much. It would have made her doubt the way I laughed when she traced a finger along the scalloped lace of my bra, or how, after I ironed her shirts, I liked leaving a blush of lipstick on those clean, starched collars. All of that was true. All of it was as much me as the secrets inside that orange crate. But Sawyer might not have believed it. My mother might have been right about all my words.

Sawyer had loved me that way for seven years when I came home and found her with my grandfather's books. It was the weekend after Thanksgiving. She'd taken down the Christmas decorations from the high shelf of the closet and had found my orange crate behind the boxes.

"I wanted to surprise you," she said. She bit her lip, a little guilty. "Thought I could get all the lights up before you came home."

I blushed to see that the books were in a different order than when I had last put them back in the crate. Sawyer had gone through them.

She caught me staring. "Sorry," she said. "I didn't mean to go looking where you didn't want me to."

"I don't care," I said. "They're just books. I never read them."

"Then why's your handwriting in them?"

I knelt on the floor to put them all back in the right order, but Sawyer took my face in her hands. I felt the familiar grain of her calluses on my cheeks, the pads of her fingers worn rougher since the first time she touched me years earlier.

"You're smart," she said, her mouth close enough to mine that I could feel its heat on my lips. "I see it."

I loved my lipstick and my rosewater as much as *todas aquellas palabras,* and I loved Sawyer more than any of it. I wanted both. I wanted my body to be soft under hers, not so full of words that I was as hard to hold in her arms as water.

But she held me a little harder, her calluses like the finest sandpaper. I imagined each of her fingertips on my tongue, rough and sweet as the husks of the lychee nuts we bought from the farmer's market on Sunday mornings. Thinking of how much the fruit inside smelled like violets on our sheets made me close my eyes. A tear fell from my lash line.

Sawyer kissed it when it was halfway down my cheek. "What else are you hiding?" she asked.

I opened my eyes and let her look at me. I did not squint to keep from her those rings around the brown of my irises. She stared into me like I was fire opal, and I knew she'd seen them, that deep blue that had first told my grandfather I was a girl for questions and words, all those words.

"Did you think I didn't know?" Sawyer asked.

She put her hands on my waist and kissed me, quickly but gently, like she was pinning me down. She wanted me, still touched me like I was as soft as wet roses, even with all those secret pages. I was a butterfly over the waters of my grandmother's homeland, and Sawyer was an ocean I could move with the flicker of my eyelashes, as easily as if they were wings.

My hand found that band of bare skin between her shirt and her jeans. My fingers brushed the knobs of her spine. The soft whistle of her breath in through her teeth gave me permission to pull her shirt away from the warmth of her back, and then her body was as open as the Ireland of those poets. Her tongue, her breasts, her thighs were salt-rose and topaz on my lips. She had irises as green as those cloud forest hummingbirds, and the black in the center of each opened and spread when she slid her hand up my skirt.

She reached between my thighs like I was her rose and she was that boy who loved me like a sky's worth of stars. She touched me like I was all petals, her fingers looking for the tight bud at the center.

She was all those words. *Todas aquellas palabras*. And I could tell her all of it, everything, as soon as I caught my breath.

GOOD GIRLS GONE BAD

Larkin Rose

Good girls did not fall in love with bad girls.

Lacy stepped back until she bumped against the wall. A picture frame rattled in protest. Liquid fire stroked her inner thighs as her pussy clenched in anticipation.

Samantha stared down at her with sea-green eyes, her short brown hair lying in sexy waves against her forehead. She licked her lips as she grabbed Lacy's hands and locked them above her head.

"I'm going to fuck you until someone calls the cops to silence your screams." She dipped and sucked at Lacy's bottom lip.

Lacy let loose a rushed gasp, arching into Sam. The woman truly knew how to make her yield to her every command. How could she allow Sam to turn her into a boneless rag doll with just a mere touch? With hot, spicy words? Wasn't she supposed to be leaving? How did Sam stop her every time, right when she was ready to slip past the door?

When Sam slid a hand between her legs, she cried out,

Goose bumps pebbled against her skin. Within minutes, she'd be coming, and screaming.

"I want you burning alive. I want your pussy to throb when you think of me. I want you to shudder every time my image crosses your mind." Sam squeezed her crotch, fanning the already blazing embers into a roaring fire. She dug her fingers harder. "When you walk out those doors, I want you to remember just what you left behind."

Lacy ground her hips toward the hand sparking heat between her legs. *Dammit,* where was her self-control? Where had Sam tossed it this time? "Please, Sam. You know I have to..."

Sam pushed her fingers deeper, choking off her words, pressing the fabric of her panties and jeans harder against the wet flesh of her pussy. Spears of pleasured pain streaked through her gut, making her nipples pebble against her lace bra. Her eyelids fluttered shut with the onslaught of lust pouring over her.

"Promise me you'll remember my touch, the way I make you feel when we make love, and every breathtaking kiss. Especially this, the way I set you on fire. I wish you could see you the way I see you. Your lips parted, your ragged breaths, your eyes full of lust and your skin pink from my lips. You'd never want yourself to leave, either."

She pulled her hand away, leaving Lacy cold, empty and out of her mind with need. Out of all of her lovers, no one had ever managed to drag such intensity from her, leave her limp.

With a groan, she peeled her eyes open to stare at Sam. Damn, she had to be the most gorgeous woman in the world. Her chiseled jaw curved down to a pointed chin. When she smiled, the cutest dimples appeared on each corner of her mouth. The love she saw staring back at her made her want to crumple to the carpet and weep like a child. Hadn't she always wanted that kind of love? The kind you never had to question? She had only to look at Sam to see the want, the need, the genuine love nestled in the depths of those eyes.

"I could never forget you."

"Promise?"

"Sam, I have to..."

"Shut up! Take off those jeans before I'm forced to spank you."

Lacy's insides quivered at the prospect of being slung over Sam's lap. Without a second's hesitation, she tugged the clasp free of her low-cut Levi's. She wiggled the denim down her hips and kicked them off. Her pale pink lace thong followed.

"What a pretty pussy you have. Now, unbutton that cute little halter."

"No. You do it."

Sam backed up, crossed her arms and smiled. That sarcastic grin made cream rush to the opening of Lacy's pussy. She was a wimp. That's all there was to it. Why couldn't she just walk out that door and ignore Sam's delays?

She huffed and fumbled with the three buttons of her shirt, opening the material for the hungry eyes devouring her. Sam knew she was putty in her hands when Lacy was horny, and wet, and being stared down like a lion's prey.

Teasingly, she dipped her finger inside the lace and lifted her breast out. She pinched her nipple and rolled it between her fingers. Tingles shot straight to her pussy. She rolled her hips, searching for satisfaction.

Sam moved forward and reached for the other breast, circling her thumb against the material, teasing her nipple into a hard bud before she tugged the lace down to expose her.

"You have the most delicious tits I've ever seen. *Playboy* should be throwing contracts your way for just a peek at this body."

Lacy rolled her tongue along the seam of her lips. "Want to taste them?"

A smile crawled along Sam's mouth as with slow, delicate movements she licked the jeweled tip, gently pulling the edge between her lips. She swirled her tongue against it and made Lacy mew like a kitten.

Lacy fisted her hands against the rush of heat and panted, "God, you drive me crazy."

Sam loosened her grip and knelt to the floor. "Spread your legs and touch yourself."

Lacy stared down at her, inching her hand over her chest and stomach to slowly slip a single finger between her wet lips.

"Flick your clit. I want to watch you come."

Lacy couldn't help but smile. What a deliciously nasty woman Sam was. The kink she'd introduced Lacy to left her weak-kneed and saturated with pleasure. No other lover could compare to what she'd found in Sam. She knew without a doubt she'd never find anyone else close to what she had right here in front of her.

She shoved the thoughts from her mind and did as she was told, spreading her lips and slowly circling the tip of her finger against her swollen tissue. Heat spread up her spine and she arched into her hand.

"Please, Sam, finish me. I have to..."

Sam leaned forward and swatted her hand out of the way. "It's not time for you to go, baby. I'm not ready to part with you."

Delicately, with a pace that sparked electricity down Lacy's legs, Sam thumbed her lips apart and swiped her tongue along her clit.

Lightning flashed behind Lacy's eyelids.

She cried out and wove her fingers into Sam's hair, pulling her face closer. "Fuck me. Oh god, Sam, fuck me!"

Sam slipped a finger inside, stroked several glorious times, and then added another, stretching against her slick walls. When she added yet another, Lacy sucked in a deep breath through clenched teeth and ground her hips first against Sam's face, then against the wall, rounding back to that torturous tongue.

Her heart swelled at the same time her orgasm climbed. This woman, this skilled lover, was more than she'd ever asked for, was never the person she was destined to find.

Good girls did not fall in love with bad girls. Lacy wasn't a good girl. She'd been a bad girl all her life, inside and out. The officers at the county jail had been on a first-name basis with her parents during her rowdy teenage years. Stealing from department stores, doing more than her share of drugs and using vehicles as her means of relieving stress by smashing windshields and headlights. Being rowdy was her style, was her forte.

The players from the football team, as well as a few naughty cheerleaders, still gave her winks if she passed them on the streets. She'd gone through them like candy, never finding a single one to simmer the coiling need inside her.

Though those days were many years behind her now, the reputation she'd gained for herself still surrounded her, still in the eyes of the older generation, the ones who remembered her wild-child life. They watched her as if she might beat up their firstborn children, or worse, fuck them. Her life had changed, though that need to be bad had plagued her throughout the years. Then she'd met a good girl. Sam. A girl who loved her family, who worshipped her friends, who wouldn't dream of raising her fist to a living soul or fucking someone just because they were there for the taking. And here Lacy was, in Sam's grasp yet again, out of her mind with need, unable to get away.

Sam…the good girl in love with Lacy, the bad girl. Sometimes, the thought was too much to handle. Who would have ever thought good girls could be so bad, or fuck so good?

Sam latched onto her clit and sucked it, stroking her fingers deep and hard inside her pussy. Lacy fisted her hands into the silky strands and tugged, pressing her head against the wall behind her. “Make me come, baby. I’m on fire.”

When the pressure against her clit ceased, she stared down at Sam. Sam withdrew her fingers and stood, leaning into Lacy. She smelled her own arousal against Sam’s lips as they crushed against her mouth, tongue delving inside, mating with her own.

Sam pulled free, raking her teeth against Lacy’s bottom lip, desire dancing in her eyes. “Turn around, baby, and bend over.”

“Sam. Please. I have...”

Sam put a finger against Lacy’s lips and whispered, “*Shh.* No, you don’t. Just a few more minutes, baby.” She grinned and grabbed Lacy’s hips, spinning her around to face the wall. “Open yourself for me.”

Lacy spread her legs and bent over, pressing her hands and cheek against the wall. When fingers probed at the slit of her pussy, she sighed, anticipation making her insides throb like a dull heartbeat. Sam’s fingers entered her, sliding into her slick depths easily, stroking out to the edge only to drive in to the hilt again, and again, and dear god, again.

Lacy lost herself in the fire scorching her from the inside out. Fire. Glorious fucking painful fire.

Sam’s free hand circled around her stomach, down between her legs. She parted Lacy’s lips and worked her clit with the tip of her finger.

“Fuck me, baby. Oh, god, I’m begging you.”

Sam obliged, pressing her hips against the back of her hand, forcing those fingers in and out of her. Lacy’s face jolted against the wall with every thrust, Sam’s hips smacking against her flesh like hand slaps. She dug her nails into the wall, grinding her teeth at the pleasure, her building orgasm ready to rob her of coherent thought.

The thrusts slowed and then stopped. Sam withdrew her fingers, then dragged them along the crack of her ass, moistening her anus. Lacy moaned and shifted her legs further apart. She should feel like a wanton hussy, ready and willing to be filled completely, but she couldn't. The orgasms were too phenomenal, and Sam was too damn good at it, never causing undue pain, only bringing out-of-this-world pleasure. Sam held the reins, making Lacy helpless, stripping her of control. She was at Sam's mercy, and worse, Sam knew it.

At the same time Sam's fingers filled Lacy's pussy again, her thumb pressed against her asshole. Lacy held her breath in anticipation of the heated sting of entrance. Instead, Sam teased her, pressing in then releasing, repeating the process until Lacy sobbed and pleaded, crying out her name in harsh breaths. Lacy arched her back and lifted her hips, begging with her movements to be fucked.

Sam lay across her back and pressed her mouth to her ear. "I love you, Lacy."

Lacy lifted her cheek away from the wall and looked over her shoulder, heart swelling to its max. God, how she loved this bad good girl.

Sam straightened and shoved her thumb inside.

Lacy whipped her head back and screamed, raking her nails against the blue paint. Thrust after thrust, Sam buried herself inside, slamming her body against Lacy's ass, all the while circling and pinching Lacy's clit into a tight ball. Stroking fire in Lacy's gut.

"Please, don't go, Lacy. Stay with me. I don't think I can live without you."

With her face bumping against the plaster, with her insides cramping into a tight knot, her orgasm teetered on the edge.

"Sam, I ..."

She didn't think those thrusts could get any deeper, but they did. They did.

"Sam!"

Sam slammed against her ass, wedging her fingers deeper inside her everywhere. The pleasure coiled tighter, stealing her sanity. The burning in her core sizzled to unbearable temperatures.

"Oh god, I'm gonna come, baby. Don't stop!" Lacy used the wall for leverage, meeting Sam's thrusts with a backward shove, making her fingers plunge inside her slippery walls.

"Come for me, baby. Scream my name. Let everyone know who you belong to."

Her orgasm catapulted over the edge. She screamed and moaned, words fracturing as pulse after pulse gripped her insides. Sam flattened her hand against her crotch, vibrating against her clit and burying her fingers until they could reach no further.

"God, I love feeling you come around my fingers. You're like the Energizer Bunny. You keep going and going and going." Sam kissed her shoulder, her harsh breaths feathering against Lacy's skin. "I'm so damn addicted to you. I think I need counseling."

Lacy snickered through gasps, her knees finally giving way. She slumped against the wall, her legs still parted.

Sam started pumping her fingers in and out again, a little trick she'd learned through their nights of sex play, and then started rubbing her clit again, slowly building up speed. As always, another orgasm raced to the edge.

Sam whispered, "I'm addicted to your orgasms, enthralled with your helpless cries. Come, baby, come."

"Oh, god, Sam!" Lacy ground her teeth as a second orgasm racked through her body. She cleaved to Sam, loving the feel of those protective arms holding her upright. Sam's heart fluttered against her back, her breaths hot against Lacy's neck.

"I agree," Lacy gasped, "you need therapy."

Light kisses trailed across her shoulders and Lacy finally regained some strength. She reached behind her, fingers searching between Sam's legs. Sam unclasped her jeans and pushed them down to her thighs. She grabbed Lacy's hand and pressed it against her crotch.

"Do you feel that? That wet heat? That's what you do to me." She pushed Lacy's fingers inside her slippery pussy and let out a moan. "You make me so fucking horny. All the time. Day and night. There's not a psychologist alive who could prevent me from reacting to you."

Lacy flicked Sam's clit with her thumb while she stroked her fingers in and out. "It's my hot animal magnetism, that's all. There's no cure for that. Sorry."

Sam ground her hips, clutching Lacy to her. "I fucking love you, Lacy. I don't care what you were or what you did before me. I'm terrified of what I might be without you."

Sam's insides pulsed, and she moaned against Lacy's back. With a loud groan, she nipped the delicate skin at the nape of Lacy's neck. Lacy's heart swelled as Sam held on to her like a life preserver, clamping her arms around her like she'd never get another chance. Sam pumped her hips to match the pulses of her orgasm, and when the tremors subsided, both women slid to the floor.

Lacy stroked Sam's hair back from her forehead and pressed her lips against her damp skin. "I have to go, Sam. You know that."

Sighing, Sam stood and clasped her pants. "I know. And you

wonder why I want to fuck you all the time. The only time I have control over you is when you're breathless and coming all over the place. You're too damn independent. Too wild. I can't tame that damn tiger any other time."

Lacy chuckled, pulled her thong and jeans back on and smoothed her hair. "You're a freak, ya know?"

"It's not my fault you come so damn good."

Lacy giggled and wrapped her arms around Sam's neck. "I'm in love with you, you weirdo." She pressed a kiss against Sam's warm lips. "Can I *please* go to the grocery store now? Your parents are going to be here in less than two hours. Your mom will kill me if I don't have her favorite red velvet cake. And god forbid I don't get that chicken cooked in time. Your dad will throw a hissy fit."

Sam gave a lazy smile. "Your alfredo sauce doesn't taste anywhere near as good as you do. Mmm mmm good." She tightened her grip. "My bad girl gone good."

Lacy snuggled into her arms. "Yeah, but my good girl is deliciously bad. And sooooo damn good at it."

MY SWEETEST NOELLE

Rebekah Weatherspoon

I fucked up. Okay, I fucked up royally. But it was too late to do anything about it. There I was in a gorgeous private condo, surrounded by the snow-capped peaks of Vail, Colorado. My baby shar-pei was asleep in my lap, laid out by a doggy biscuit–induced coma. *Home Alone* was just warming up on USA. Our tree was decorated, white lights twinkling, and my girlfriend was two thousand miles away. On Christmas Eve.

I wasn't going to cry. I would not do it. I wasn't going to call her back either. She'd made up her mind to leave. Yeah, I hadn't really helped things along. I was a total bitch when she told me what her mother had wanted. I walked right over to my laptop, whipped out my credit card and booked her a ticket right back to Connecticut so she could spend Christmas with her family. Instead of with me.

I understood what she was dealing with. We both came from pretty conservative families, but I'd given my parents the ultimatum the moment Noelle and I had decided to see each other exclusively. Love me, love Noelle. No exceptions. It took my mother a little while to get used to the fact that I was lesbian. My father couldn't give less of a shit. His politico buddies and golf partners would only care if he had a gay son, and my packing up Noelle and moving across the country kept my sexuality out of their dinner parties and church functions. My parents were supportive from a distance and luckily stayed the hell out of my business.

Noelle's mother was a different story.

She was on marriage number four. A ridiculously rich bank tycoon whom she'd met at a charity event for some disease no one she actually knew had. Noelle was her oldest and her only normal child. The only child she claimed had been born out of love, the only one who hadn't been to rehab, hadn't been arrested or knew not to bring up husbands one through three in mixed company just to get a rise out of mommy dearest.

This Christmas was the first with her new, richest husband to date. There were guests to be entertained, another charity function to host, a holiday ball to attend, and the Lady Madam Susan Bishop-Klein-Swathmore-Crane wanted her most competent, most articulate child by her side so she could at least pretend she knew the meaning of family during this symbolic time of year.

Noelle could have said no. She could have offered up a big ole *Pass, maybe next year* like I had done with my parents. They were into the same crap, just in a different state, but my mother liked the sauce and liked to embarrass me in front of company once the vodka tonics started flowing.

For some reason, Noelle could never say no to her mother. Maybe it was some sense of familial obligation or maybe Noelle actually felt bad for the woman. The Grand Duchess of Crane was pretty pathetic, and never kept many friends—or husbands.

Her other children hated her. Either way, Noelle had a heart the size of the moon, and whenever her mother wanted to see her, even if it was just to show her off as social eye candy, Noelle couldn't turn her down. So off she scampered for the occasional Easter, the random Fourth of July, which was all fine and good, but Christmas? Come on.

I didn't even care that Susan Crane didn't like me. I took good care of Noelle. I had a degree. I owned the most successful salon in Beverly Hills. Bought it out from under my boss before the thirty candles on my last cake had even cooled. It would have made a little sense, well, no sense at all, but more sense if she wasn't cool with the fact that I was a proud Latina or that I took almost equal pride in my Monroe piercing. But no. All that mattered to her was that five- to eight-inch thing that didn't dangle just below my hips, that I *wasn't* a man.

You'd think I'd turned Noelle gay, which was another layer of bullshit. Noelle was busy playing "Show Me Yours" with the girls at her boarding school way before we met, but after we moved in together her mother realized her daughter's love for pussy, salsa and merengue wasn't a phase. We already told the lady we'd give her grandkids using Noelle's perfectly viable eggs and all. I loved Noelle and I would take care of her as long as we were together. I wasn't going to beg the lady to accept our relationship, and I wasn't going to grow a dick. There was nothing else she was getting from me.

See, I think people, including her mother, always assumed I was with Noelle for superficial reasons. It wasn't my fault that she was banging hot with the juiciest tits I'd ever seen, that she had an ass that should be against the law in any state with crosswalks. Those were factors that I loved, and not even as much as I loved her pussy. Always waxed to perfection, soft and blushing pink. Always wet for me. She tasted so sweet, and the noises she made when she was trying not to come just because she wanted the attention I was paying between her legs to last—damn. I could go down on Noelle for hours. My hips squirmed in the couch cushions just from the thought of eating her out.

Her stunning body and my now-damp underwear aside, her smile was the element of her beauty that won me over, and this impossible ability she had to love that made me stay. Susan Crane had no idea what kind of child she'd birthed into this world, how unbelievably amazing Noelle was. Everyone who saw her art was affected by it. Impossible not to be. But there was so much more to her than her talent with a brush. She lived to help others, volunteered her ass off in her free time. Kids, animals, the homeless, war vets. If Noelle could find them, she'd help them, and not just by writing a check.

God, if Susan would just look at her daughter, just see her once for who she was—a sweet, intelligent angel—she'd know that whoever made her happy was good enough.

I was there for Noelle when her father died. I was there when she realized she needed to chase her art and not a law degree. I was there through the nights of self-doubt, the days where she couldn't get a gallery to take her seriously. And the best part of it all, I was there when Noelle sold her first piece. I got to see that smile. I got that first hug, was nearly made deaf by that first squeal of joy. I was there for her, not her mother. And where was Noelle now? With her mother.

And now I felt like an idiot. I should have just stayed home. I'd spent a hunk of cash on this condo, with its private hot tub and fireplace and its enormous bed. I'd paid extra to have a healthy little tree brought in, and even though I hated skiing, I'd booked a lift package for the whole week, all for Noelle. We'd ski, we'd fuck and on Christmas morning I was going to ask her to marry me. It was the perfect plan, until Bitch à la Crane called.

There was an unspoken rule that I wasn't welcome to represent myself as anything other than Noelle's "friend" within a fifty-mile radius of her mother or anyone who knew her. Noelle did that adorable lip quiver thing she does when she got off the phone, but I said no. I wasn't going. We wouldn't be allowed to sleep in the same room. I wouldn't be allowed to touch her in public without her mother going ape shit. I refused to spend my holidays that way. So I pouted and sulked the whole week before she left. I considered making up with her, a little peace offering and a pledge that I still loved her even if her mother was cunt of the year, and then she made an appointment at my salon.

All hell would have broken loose if she'd gone somewhere else, I'll give her that, but I'd spent hours dying her soft brown hair this kick-ass combination of jet black and royal blue and she just comes walking in the door, asking Carlo to take her somewhere north of blond, with a lot of highlights. To say I was pissed would be a weak way to express how I really felt. I was livid, more so because she actually looked sexy as fuck as a blonde. I got to secretly enjoy the new look for a whole twenty-four hours before she slipped out of my life.

I may have been a brat and hidden her present in her luggage as a long-distance "F U for leaving me." Then I sent her to the airport alone. To pour a little extra piss in the vinegar, I'd emailed her yesterday, telling her exactly where I was going. I may have included a link to the resort complete with pictures of the mountain and all our condo's amenities. Okay, yeah. I was being a huge bitch, but *who* ditches their girlfriend on Christmas?

She'd called and texted few times since she'd left, when Susan wasn't looking, of course. She'd been blowing up my phone on and off all day. I'd been too busy playing with the dog, Noelle's "Here, have a puppy so you won't be completely alone on the holidays" parting gift. I would have been really mad if the dog wasn't so damn cute. I'd been talking about getting a shar-pei for years, and did Noelle deliver. Little Prince Michael was the only thing keeping me from a crying jag and case of wine.

My bit of John Hughes heaven went to commercial and suddenly that little black box on the coffee table had my attention. I picked it up and flicked the lid open. One solitary diamond secured in a thick platinum band. I was still gonna ask her. I loved her too much to want her as anything less than my wife, but we had to do something about her mother and then I had to plan another romantic weekend to get down on one knee.

I should have asked her to stay. I should have done a lot of things differently, but it really was too late. I was already showered and changed for bed. I'd already binged on the resort's four-star cuisine. I'd finish my movie and fuck myself to sleep. In the morning, maybe I'd just go home.

A little growly whimper in my lap made me jump and then I heard boot steps on the stairs. Prince Michael yelped this time as a light knock sounded on the door. For a moment my chest cramped with irrational fear. People didn't just show up at your door at this hour, and I hadn't called for room service. I stood and tucked PM under my arm, ignoring his attempts to gnaw on my thumb. Just then the doorbell rang.

"Who is it?" I yelled in my most threatening, scary tone.

A tiny voice came through the thick panel of wood. "Ronnie?"

"Shit. Shit!" I was halfway across the room when I realized I'd left her ring right out in the open. I dropped the dog on the floor, then practically dove for it. I threw the little box in my purse before I booked it back to the door. I swung it open and there was my baby on the other side. Standing in the cold. Crying her eyes out.

I couldn't hold in my gasp. I'd never seen her looking so upset before, never seen her looking so beautiful either, her gorgeous face all pink and blotchy—partly from the wind, I'm guessing, and partly from the tears. Fat snowflakes stuck to her hair and her down jacket, refusing to melt.

She hiccupped, her adorable button lip quivering. She held a box of hair dye in her bare hand, Raven Black No. 21. "Can you dye my hair back?"

"Baby." I grabbed her and pulled her inside, out of the cold.

"I'm sorry," she sobbed. I shook my head, begging her to stop apologizing. I'd already forgotten everything that had happened. I didn't care anymore why she'd left and when. All I wanted to know was what had brought her back and what the hell had made her cry.

I grabbed her cheeks and kissed her full on her soft pink lips. She dropped her bag and the box of dye right there on the floor and kissed me back just as desperately. After a moment, I pulled away with a shiver. I could feel the cold night air all over her.

"God. You're freezing."

"I was waiting for a cab forever," she sniffled. I unzipped her jacket and watched her as she pulled it off. She toed out of her big boots, making us the same height again, then let me tug her to the couch. I ignored how cold her jeans were against my flannel-covered legs and threw a fuzzy plaid blanket over us both. Then I just held her with her cool cheek tucked against my neck and rocked her and kissed her until she stopped trembling, until the tears started to slow.

Finally she gazed up at me with her wide brown eyes, now all bloodshot and puffy. This had to have been an all-day episode. She'd never even bothered with makeup, not that she needed any.

"I missed you so much," she whispered. Before I could tell

her how much *she* had been missed, Noelle kissed me. Slower this time than the kiss we'd shared at the door, letting me feel that my attempts at sharing some warmth were working. The tip of her tongue teased me gently with light flicks over my upper lip. My lungs released a deep breath that brushed across her mouth as a long sigh. I'd just let her play as she wanted. I'd give her anything to make the crying stop completely, and she was making me so wet I'd be a fool to tell her to explain first.

I shifted my weight and pulled her closer into my lap. The taste of her tears mixed with the subtle hint of lip balm as I kissed her deeper. My nipples came to life against the cold knit of her sweater, but it was being with Noelle that made my sensitive buds hard. Having her near me again made my whole body tingle and ache.

We both broke away when a familiar yipping noise from the floor brought us back to reality. Prince Michael was feeling a little left out. I scooped him up and nestled him in the blanket between us, petting the soft gray fur around his face.

"What happened?" I asked gently.

"Hi, Blanket." She ignored my question, choosing to play with PM's wrinkled belly instead. I wanted to be patient with her, but now I had to know.

"Noelle. Please tell me what happened."

She sighed, then looked me in the eye. I knew this couldn't be good. My girl was a chatterbox. She only hesitated when she had news that would piss me the hell off. "So...we had that ball last night and you remember that guy Preston Tripbeck?"

"Yeah." The poster child for all that was wrong with yuppie America.

"Well, Mother had him seated next to me, and he was acting all nice and normal. Then he fucking kissed me."

My mind short-circuited for a moment, but when it came

back online it still hadn't fully processed what she had just told me. My body understood this shitty news just fine, though. A sinking feeling made room for a huge lump in my stomach and heat shot up my spine, across the back of my head.

"Wait. What? Go back. He kissed you at the dinner table."

"No. Sorry. He asked me to dance and I figured sure. It's the waltz. He's not asking me to bend over so he can shove bills in my G-string. So we were dancing and he made some joke about how we should start calling a square dance just to break up the monotony. So I laughed 'cause it was funny and he just kissed me. He wasn't fresh with his hands or anything, so I didn't slap him."

My confusion and my anger were in a very heated argument. At the moment it felt like it would be a draw. "He kissed you?" I asked again hesitantly.

She swallowed and looked down at her hands. Another thing I had to blame Susan for. Noelle always thought everything was her fault. "Yeah."

I wasn't angry with her. I was pissed at Preston. Noelle was charming as hell, but she wasn't a flirt and she wasn't a tease. Screw all the mixed signals in the world, he had no right to touch her. And yes, *I* was the poster child for jealousy. I took a deep breath and kissed her cheek. She sighed a bit, melting into me. I traced the back of her hand as she traced our puppy's fur. She'd only been gone three days, but I'd missed those soft, strong hands and all the amazing things they could do. I kissed her again.

"I told him I was seeing someone and he apologized, but the rest of the night was awkward as hell."

"Then what, baby?"

"God. So this morning, Judith, the housekeeper, wakes me up telling me I have a call. It was Preston, and he says Mother told him I was single and interested in him, but I was just shy about making any advances. I cleared things up right then and he apologized like ten times."

Okay, maybe he wasn't all bad.

"But when I came down for breakfast Mother threw a fit and told me I had just ruined things. I couldn't even—I just left. Well, I charged my ticket on her card and then I left. I told her I'd be back when she accepts me for who I am and who I love."

My head snapped back at her serious tone and the giggle that followed. "Bullshit. You did not."

Noelle smiled. "I did. Alexander just snorted. He didn't even look up from his paper. I kinda think he's on my side. Anyway. Screw her. I love you and I'm sorry."

"Why doesn't she—how…" I bit back my insults. "*I'm* sorry you had to deal with that. And I'm sorry for being such a bitch. I should have answered my phone. You could have been hurt. I mean, you were, and I won't do that again."

"You had every right to. I just, I left you for nothing. Really, though, can you dye my hair back?"

"Yes, baby." I laughed, tucking her long bangs back behind her ear. "You know I will. Not using that box shit, but when we get home I'll fix it. Are you hungry?"

"I'm starving, but I want to shower first. I feel so gross." She stood up and got her first glimpse at the living room. The tree. The festive little doggy bed I'd picked up for Prince Michael. The fireplace with a strategically placed faux-fur rug.

Noelle turned back to me, her eyes glistening again. "You did all this for us?"

"For you, yeah."

She looked away again, hiding more tears, I guessed. I jumped up from the couch, keeping the puppy in my grip, and walked right to her. Gently, I swept my thumb under her eyes while cradling the baby-soft skin of her face. Prince Michael helped by licking her chin affectionately. "Hey. None of that. You're here now, and Blanket won't need to go out for another three hours. That's what matters."

"I love you," she murmured again.

I would never get tired of hearing those words from her. It was so clear then. This was perfection. My perfect little family. "Hold that thought." I set Blanket down on the floor and walked toward my purse.

"What—"

I reached over the couch and grabbed the velvet box out of my bag. She knew me. I knew her. We didn't need any more dramatics tonight.

The small hinges protested silently as I pulled back the lid. I could feel her eyes on me as I turned the box toward her and placed it in her upturned palm. I gave her a moment to stare at the sizable diamond before I popped the actual question.

"Marry me."

"You planned all this...for *this*?" Her eyes popped wide.

"Yes. Please, Noelle. I love you and I want to be with you forever."

"Forever?" she said, suddenly bashful. "Me, you and puppy?"

"Well, I hope our marriage lasts longer than the dog, but yeah—"

"Veronica!"

"—That's the idea."

My Noe looked back down at the ring. The most gorgeous smile spread across her face. The blindingly beautiful smile I'd seen the first day we met, the one I hoped I would see through many Christmas nights to come.

Two fat tears rolled down her cheeks. She looked at me, back down at the ring, then met my nervous gaze again. "Yes. Oh, my god, yes. Yes. Yes."

"Really?" I had no idea where the sudden wave of insecurity came from.

Noelle pulled the ring out of the box and slid it right on her left hand. "Yes."

I didn't know what else to say but "Thank you."

"You're so silly." She threw her arms around my neck. Twice she kissed me softly, pulling my bottom lip between hers, before she said with a devious little smile, "So since you asked me, I guess I'll be taking your last name."

"Oh, your mom will love that."

"I know, right?" She kissed me again, pressing her hips against mine. My clit flexed and shuddered at the sensation. "Come shower with me."

"Nope."

She gasped, mocking me with her exaggerated shock. I chuckled and took a playful nip at her neck. Her gasp this time sounded more like a moan.

"You go up." I nibbled her skin again. "Take your time and I'll order you some dinner."

Noelle leaned back, flashing that heart-racing smile, the one that pulled all her innocence and sex appeal right to the surface. "And then you'll eat my pussy?"

"There's the dirty girl I love."

This kiss was hard and fast. "The dirty girl you're gonna marry."

THE PORTRAIT

D. Jackson Leigh

I swear I never saw it coming. Sure, things haven't been that good in the bedroom for us in a while, but I've been building a business and I had surgery and my sister was sick—"

"And your dog died, your daddy went to prison and your mama got run over by a train," Mick finished for her friend Diane.

Diane looked up from the designs she was drawing in her refried beans. "Asshole."

Mick and Diane had been friends since college, but enough was enough. "It's been a year, buddy. You need to get over Cheryl." Mick softened her voice. "Have you thought about seeing someone professionally to talk about it?"

"Go see a shrink? Hell no." Diane threw her napkin onto her plate. "Didn't know I was being a nuisance. I'll shut up about it."

"Come on, I'm serious. This is...what...your sixth live-in relationship? Maybe it wouldn't hurt to figure out what you're doing wrong...whether it's picking the wrong women or leaving the cap off the toothpaste."

"So, you finally admit that you think it was my fault."

"Listen to yourself, Diane. You're the one who said Cheryl tried to tell you she was unhappy. All she wanted was for you to—"

"The only thing I did wrong with Cheryl was believe her when she said that young bitch hanging around her was just a friend."

As much as she loved her buddy, Mick had listened to the same tirade a million times.

Diane stopped and narrowed her eyes at Mick's impatient sigh. "Maybe you should listen to yourself for a change."

"What are you talking about?" Mick said.

"I'm talking about that new neighbor you have, the hot young artist who's been hovering around Sophie for the past two months."

Mick slid forward in her chair and pointed a finger at Diane. "Don't even go there. I trust Sophie implicitly."

"Uh-huh. How much time have you spent with her lately?"

"I'm an accountant and we just finished tax season. We've been together almost twenty-five years. Sophie knows what tax season is like by now."

"Bet Miss Hottie doesn't have to worry about tax season."

Mick stood. "I know you're still hurt over Cheryl. That's the only reason I'm not going to punch your lights out and tell Sophie what you've insinuated about her." She threw some money on the table to pay for her lunch. "Get some help, Diane."

Mick studied her reflection in the plate glass that was the back wall of her fifth-floor office. When did those lines appear around her mouth? Sophie said they were frown lines. Mick raised the corners of her mouth to make them disappear, but her smile looked more like a grimace and accentuated the crow's feet around her eyes. She had considered dying her short, spiky hair when it turned snow white, but Sophie refused. It was the perfect contrast to Mick's blue eyes, she insisted.

Mick still felt the same as she did when she was thirty. But the person looking back at her was old. Too old to have a lover fifteen years younger. Despite her adamant rejection of Diane's implication, the seed of doubt had been planted, its roots taking hold in Mick's thoughts all afternoon.

She sighed and turned away from her introspection. It was only four o'clock, but Sophie had warned her not to be late coming home tonight. It was Mick's sixtieth birthday. Damn it. She didn't want to have another birthday. She wanted time to stand still for her but let Sophie catch up. She wanted to be the gracious one, the one to laugh and say, "I love every line in your face." At least she had talked Sophie out of throwing a big party like she did for Mick's fiftieth.

She started to toss a few files into her briefcase, then thought better of it. No taking work home tonight. And, damn it, she'd take the stairs this time. Old, out-of-shape people rode the elevator. She grabbed her keys and punched the office intercom.

"Rachel, I'm gone for the day...going out the back way."

"I'll call Sophie so she'll have time to chase the naked women out of the house." The office's receptionist's standard reply was an old joke from the time Sophie had to teach a body sculpture class in her home studio because the college wouldn't allow nude models. Mick usually laughed, but today it settled like soured milk on her stomach.

"I'm talking about that new neighbor you have, the hot young artist who's been hovering around Sophie for the past two months."

Mick shook the thought from her head. That was just stupid. She pushed the door open and headed for the Toyota in her reserved parking space. Maybe she'd go car shopping this weekend and buy that BMW convertible she'd always wanted. Yeah. Why not? A present to herself. They could afford it. Her mood suddenly lighter, Mick revved up the Camry, turned off the air conditioner and rolled the windows down. It wasn't a convertible, but the wind blowing through her hair felt satisfyingly reckless.

Mick breezed through the house with a grin on her face. It was her birthday, after all, and she planned to cash in on that. Her. Sophie. Naked.

Her smile disappeared when she pushed open the door to the studio. Sophie wasn't alone. Garrett, the studly artist who had recently moved next door, huddled close as they murmured over something in Sophie's sketchbook.

"What's so interesting?" Mick growled.

Sophie slapped the sketchbook shut and stood. "Hey, honey. You're early, aren't you?"

Mick pulled Sophie to her, pressed their hips together and kissed her possessively. "It's my birthday. I get anything I want on my birthday, right? That includes coming home early and ravishing my sexy wife, doesn't it?"

Sophie glanced at Garrett and laughed nervously, pushing against Mick's shoulders. "Slow down, tiger. Garrett needs a favor before you start unwrapping birthday gifts."

Garrett gave Sophie a conspiratorial look. "I apologize for delaying your birthday plans, but we're only talking about a few minutes."

Mick frowned. Exactly what was she implying would take only a few minutes, the favor or Mick's seduction?

"Go on," Sophie said. "Garrett can't figure out the controls on the whirlpool tub and I need to get cleaned up before we can go to dinner."

Mick moved her hands down and gave Sophie's butt a squeeze. "When I get back, we'll review what's on the menu."

Sophie blushed and glanced over at Garrett again. "I need at least twenty minutes to get ready."

Mick impatiently followed as Garrett casually sauntered to the house next door. The Tudor-style brick house was a third larger than her and Sophie's house. Garrett had moved in two months before and quickly bonded with Sophie when they realized they were both artists.

"So, I know you're an artist, but how do you make your living? Do you teach somewhere like Sophie?" Surely Garrett had some young students who were more interesting than Mick's wife.

"No. I seriously doubt I'd have the patience for teaching. I paint portraits."

"Really. Sophie hates painting portraits. Says it's too boring."

Garrett turned to Mick and smiled. "I suppose a lot of people think that. I like the challenge of finding that characteristic that makes each individual unique and figuring out how to make it shine through in the painting."

"I'm not sure what you mean."

"Like a 'tell' gives away what someone's thinking during a poker game. Let me see if I can come up with a good example." Garrett was silent as she led Mick upstairs to the extravagant bathroom of the master suite and turned toward the huge mirror over the double vanity. "A mentor pointed out to me that I tend to talk with my body more than most people...the set of my shoulders is indicative of my mood, I cock my head when I'm thinking, tuck my chin and look up through my eyelashes when I'm aroused, thrust my chin out when I feel threatened. A good portrait painter should be able to capture that."

Could this woman be more self-absorbed?

Garrett gestured toward the mirror. "What about yourself? What would someone need to see to paint you effectively?"

Mick shrugged as she surveyed the pinstripes in her white shirt that matched her neatly pressed black Dockers. "I just see me. I don't spend a lot of time looking at myself in the mirror." Technically, the window in her office wasn't a mirror.

Garrett chuckled. "A necessity of my occupation, I'm afraid." She eyed Mick. "Okay. Let's try someone you do look at often. Sophie's tell is her lips. She purses her lips when she's thinking. She pokes them out in a pout when she's not happy. She chews her bottom lip when she's nervous. She stretches them in a thin line when she's pissed."

"You've been looking at my wife's lips?"

"Down, girl. As a professional portrait painter, I can't help noticing things about almost everyone I spend time around."

Mick didn't want to think about how much time Garrett had been spending with Sophie. She wanted to be done with this pesky neighbor, go home and lay clear claim to her wife. "You needed help with the whirlpool?"

Garrett pressed the buttons on the tub's controls. Not a ripple in the water. "I called the realtor and she said everything was checked out before the sale. I checked the breaker in the fuse box and it's definitely in the 'on' position. Sophie said you helped the previous owner with the same problem, but she couldn't remember what you did to fix it."

"There's a safety cutoff in the bedroom closet that keeps you from accidentally turning the jets on and burning up the pump when there's no water. It was probably switched off when they drained the tub to inspect it before you closed on the house."

Mick went to the closet and flipped the switch, then returned to the bathroom to punch the control. The water churned.

"Great! Thanks, Mick."

"Not a problem. Planning to share this tub with someone special?" *Like a young, sexy girlfriend who isn't already in a committed partnership next door?*

"Nope. Just me and my sore back."

Mick didn't care about Garrett's sore back. "Well, I've got a hot date with more than a tub tonight and I don't want to keep her waiting."

"Let me at least offer you a beer for helping me out. Sophie said you're something of a beer connoisseur, and I have some great dark ales."

"Maybe some other time."

Mick hurried back and quietly let herself into the house. She was hoping to surprise Sophie in mid-dress so she wouldn't fuss about ruining her makeup when Mick tossed her on the bed and cashed in on her birthday. She'd show her that this sixty-year-old could still serve up hot monkey sex. She didn't need some young stud from next door. But as she approached their bedroom, she heard Sophie talking in a low voice.

"No, it's fine. I don't think she noticed, and I've got it covered up now. Thanks, Garrett. That was smart of you to plan ahead for a distraction if she ever caught us by surprise. I know. Soon. I wanted to, before her birthday, but I need more time. Thank you for being so patient. This means so much to me. I know. Bye."

Mick's stomach churned. What was Sophie covering up? They never kept secrets from each other. What was Garrett being patient about? It was pretty obvious, wasn't it? Diane was right. Something was going on, and Garrett wanted Sophie to admit it to Mick.

Her biggest fear, the one buried so deep even she hadn't realized she harbored it, was that at some point the gap between their ages was going to make a difference. She was sixty. Sophie was a young forty-five. When she hit seventy, Sophie would be a very datable fifty-five. After nearly twenty-five years together, their time was coming to an end.

Her vision swam and she caught herself against the wall as her knees buckled. God, she was going to pass out. She whirled and stumbled down the hall, crashing into a table in the foyer. The sculpture she gave Sophie for their tenth anniversary crashed to the floor, shattering along with Mick's life.

"Mick! Honey, are you okay?"

Mick steadied herself against the wall and stared down at the pieces of vase scattered across the Italian tile. She jerked away when Sophie reached for her hand. "I heard you." She choked on the words, her voice but a hoarse whisper.

Sophie froze. "You heard what?"

Mick stepped over the mess to put some distance between her and Sophie. She crossed her arms tightly over her chest, trying desperately to hold the shards of her heart together. "I heard you talking to that neighborhood Romeo, the one who's over here every time I call home from work. The one you were cuddled up with in your studio when I got home today. The one you were just whispering to on the phone." Her hurt, her anger, her voice rose with each sentence.

"Neighborhood Romeo?" Sophie threw back her head and laughed.

To Mick's dismay, her eyes filled with tears. The Sophie she knew would never be so callous. Had she changed this much while Mick had her head buried in tax returns?

She clinched her jaw against the sob that was rising up in her throat. Garrett might have stolen her wife, but Mick wouldn't surrender her dignity, too. She jammed her hands in her pockets, her fingers finding her car keys. She had to get away. She turned and strode through the house toward the garage. She made it to the kitchen before Sophie nearly tackled her, wrapping her arms tightly around Mick from behind.

"Mick, sweetheart, slow down. Wait."

"I can't...I can't do this."

"Oh my god. You're shaking."

Sophie loosened her hold to slip in front of Mick and gaze up at her. Mick stared at the floor, afraid of what she'd see if she looked into Sophie's dark chocolate eyes. Sophie gave her a little shake. Her voice was soft. "Michelle Louise Sanderson. I'd smack you if you weren't so seriously upset. First of all, I was *not* cuddled up with Garrett. We were discussing a sketch."

"Right. That's why you both jumped like two kids with their hands in the cookie jar and scrambled to hide what you were looking at. You always let me see your sketches."

"Stop interrupting me." Sophie met Mick's glare for a long moment. "Secondly, Garrett has never, ever, said or done anything inappropriate. We're friends, colleagues in our profession."

Sophie's hands were warm on Mick's cheeks. "Finally, even if she had, I would have immediately set her straight." Her lips brushed against Mick's. "You are the one I love, the center of my life."

Mick struggled to let go of the brooding doubts that plagued. "Then what were you whispering about on the phone? Why did I have to go next door on some lame mission to fix the stupid hot tub?"

Sophie didn't answer. Instead, she took Mick's hand and led

her through the house to the master bathroom. A soft piano concerto and honeysuckle-scented bathwater permeated the room, which was alight with dozens of candles.

Sophie turned and began to slowly unbutton Mick's shirt. "This is why I needed you to leave the house. To prepare the first part of your birthday gift."

Mick was speechless. How in the world had she gotten to this point, accusing this woman she had trusted, loved all these years?

Sophie had changed out of the jeans and old oxford shirt of Mick's that she wore when she painted and donned a dark blue fleece robe. Mick shrugged out of her shirt and bra and reached for the robe's tie. She slid her hands inside and pulled Sophie against her bare chest. She tasted Sophie's mint tea as she claimed those expressive lips with her mouth, her tongue.

Sophie broke their kiss and pushed Mick's pants down her hips. Her robe joined Mick's pants on the floor. "God, I love your ass."

Sophie led Mick to the tub, lowered herself into the heated, swirling water and motioned for Mick to sit between her legs. Mick did as she bid, settling her back against Sophie's full breasts. She closed her eyes and moaned as Sophie planted tiny kisses along her neck and sucked at her pulse. A rough pinch of her rock-hard nipples sent a ball of fire straight to her clit. Sophie knew every sensitive part of her body, every trigger that drove her arousal, as only a longtime lover could.

She slid lower in the water and lolled her head against Sophie's shoulder. Sophie soaped her hands and smoothed them along Mick's arms, across her chest and down her belly. Mick opened her legs to welcome the questing hands. She captured Sophie's mouth again as Sophie painted her swelling clit with the arousal pooling between her thighs—sure brushstrokes on a canvas.

Still raw from the emotion of her earlier turmoil, Mick built quickly to a climax, too quickly, and she pulled Sophie's hand away. She needed more. She needed to sooth the lingering wounds of her doubt. She burned to reassert her claim. Abruptly rising, she grabbed a thick towel.

Sophie looked startled. "Mick, what's wrong?"

"Stand up."

Confusion played across Sophie's delicate features, but she obeyed.

Mick wound the towel around Sophie and lifted her into her arms. Once in the bedroom, she gently laid her on the bed.

Sophie's knowing smile confirmed no words were needed. Opening the towel and her legs, she said, "Yours. Only yours."

"Yes." Mick hurried to take the offering. She lathed her tongue through Sophie's slick folds until the telltale tremble of her thighs vibrated against Mick's ears. Thankful for her lithe, limber lover, Mick pushed Sophie's knees to her chest and moved up to rub her clit against Sophie's drenched sex. Still swollen from Sophie's touch, Mick thrust slowly at first. She wanted to make this last. But her need was too great, her climax too close.

"Touch yourself," she whispered hoarsely, rolling her hips harder, faster as Sophie complied.

"That's it, sweetheart." Sophie gasped, her heels pressing into Mick's ass. "Almost there. Come with me."

Mick thrust wildly, urgently, sweat trickling down her jaw. She cried out as her orgasm swarmed through her. "Mine, Sophie. Mine."

"Yes, yes. Yours." Sophie bucked against her and Mick thrust her fingers inside to stroke her to a second wave of spasms.

When Mick rolled onto her back, her heart pounding, Sophie cuddled against her to trace soothing circles on her belly. Quiet while Mick's heart slowed to a normal rhythm, Sophie was the first to speak. "Are we okay?"

The tentative question tore at Mick's heart. She closed her eyes, ashamed that she had accused this beautiful woman of betraying her.

"I'm an idiot." She stroked Sophie's smooth back. "It's just... our age difference hasn't bothered me until now. For Christ's sake, my hair is completely white and you don't have a single strand of gray."

Sophie rose up on her elbow to hold Mick's gaze. "I'm a redhead. So was my mother, and she was seventy-two when she found her first gray hair. You, on the other hand, were prematurely white-headed when I met you. It didn't matter then and it doesn't matter now. I love your hair."

"Cheryl left Diane for a younger woman."

Sophie snorted. "I should have known Diane had something to do with this bout of insecurity. Age wasn't the problem between those two, and you know it."

Mick frowned. "I'm getting wrinkles."

"So am I, honey. Haven't you noticed?"

Mick studied Sophie's face. "Laugh lines. I love your laugh lines."

Tears filling her eyes, Sophie laid her hand over Mick's heart. "Do you know what scares *me* about our age difference?"

"What?"

"I am terrified of the day that I may have to come home to an empty house because you've left this life and me behind."

"Sophie, babe—"

"No. It's just something I have to accept, like you need to accept that I will love you every day until then and even in death." She wiped at her eyes and smiled. "I can't stop us from aging, honey, but I can do something about your doubts."

Sophie stood and pulled Mick to her feet. Still naked, Mick followed her into the studio to stand before a cloth-draped easel.

"When you came home early this afternoon, Garrett was going over some sketches she's been helping me with. Sketches I made to paint this for you," she said, motioning toward the easel. "It's taking longer than I thought to get it right, so instead of giving it to you for your birthday, I was going to shoot for our twenty-fifth anniversary next month." She pulled the sheet away and dropped it to the floor.

Mick stared at a handsome likeness of herself. She recognized it from a photograph taken when they'd celebrated their tenth anniversary by spending a month in the Bahamas. She was in sore need of a haircut and her windswept locks gave her a rakish look as she stared up at the camera, her eyes a piercing blue against her dark tan.

She unconsciously pulled Sophie back against her, wrapping her in a loose embrace that mirrored the portrait. It was so lifelike, she could almost smell the cocoa butter of the sunscreen they had worn.

"Oh, babe." Mick's throat tightened around the words. In the picture, Sophie was looking up at her, rather than at the camera, her gaze so tender, so adoring it made Mick ache. "I was still young then."

"And I was thinner."

"You haven't changed at all."

Sophie turned in her arms. "I have Mick. Look again."

Mick tore her eyes from the painting to gaze down at Sophie. "I am looking. I see the same girl in that portrait."

"And when I look at you, I still see the handsome woman who made love to me on that beach. That's because we see each other with our hearts, not our eyes, sweetheart. I hope that we always will."

Mick hugged Sophie tight against her and stared at the painting again. "You're an incredible artist."

"I'm good, but I don't have much experience with portraits. Garrett helped me paint what was in my heart."

"I know I was being foolish earlier, but do we have to talk about Garrett while we're naked?"

Sophie chuckled. "No, we don't. But in the future, if something is bothering you, I want you to talk to me, not bottle it up until you start listening to Diane." Her hand feathered against Mick's cheek. "Do you have anything else on your mind I should know about?"

Mick nodded and buried her face against Sophie's neck, inhaling the sweet honeysuckle scent that lingered from their bath. "A red BMW convertible."

HEARTFIRST

Kiki DeLovely

I don't know if I've ever witnessed anything more sexy than the intent and intensity in her eyes as she shakes her head, slowly, side to side, when what she really means is "Fuck, yes." As though she's disbelieving of just how incredibly right it is. As if everything about me is so right that it's wrong. She takes her sweet time with that simple motion, as if she hasn't the slightest need to rush, despite the fact that other parts of her may in fact be moving at much greater velocities. This apparent discord—between both the unspoken verbal and the pace of the physical—although seemingly misaligned, has a radical effect on my desire and even brings an asymmetrical balance to my lust. Allowing my passion to course wildly through my mind and, hence, my body—blood pounding like the stomp of wild ponies through my veins and racing to deliver an aching throb of need to my cunt.

Even after centuries of playing at this game, she still has this madness-making ability to cut me to my core with very little effort.

We're surrounded by people, all of us waiting to be seated, but once she's locked me in her gaze, all I can see is her. And she knows it. She takes a long, slow gander at me—eyeing my feet dangling on the last rung of the bar stool, trailing up my unladylike-positioned legs, fixating briefly on the lacy frill at the hem of my skirt (just long enough to lick her lips), before continuing upward. I wrap one of my patent leather heels around the back of her leg, innocent enough for general public purposes, and pull her in closer to me. She blinks her eyelids shut a little too long and inhales deeply. A lecherous grin creeps across her mouth, into her eyes. I know this look.

Leaning into my face, she pauses for several seconds—my heartbeat quickens in my clit—then makes her way to my ear. "You know that intoxicating scent of yours?" She waits just a beat for her rhetorical question to sink in and then continues, "I can smell you from here." My blush is hard and immediate, my mind racing, wondering if she can smell my cunt in a crowd of people, who else can? And yet, not caring in the slightest—feeling so gorgeous and cherished in that moment—so very pleased to please her with my scent alone.

Back home I close the door behind us and she doesn't make me wait—thank heavens she doesn't make me. No romantic foreplay, no taking her sweet time, no making love to the goddess inside me. No. Thank my luckiest stars. No, she shoves inside me fast and hard. Faster. And harder. In and out. And in. And out. So many times, so fucking fast, I feel like I'm about to lose my mind. She's been traveling for work the past month and knows I've been needing this too damn long to have to wait even a split second longer to have her. So she pounds away at my cunt like she wants to break me in two. Like a rapacious beast without the slightest inhibition. And I thank the planets for aligning our worlds, time and time again, calling forth this limitless ravishing.

She slides two of her free fingers into my mouth and I begin to suck. As I take it, she grunts out of euphoria but still wants more. Plunging them deeper down my throat, further until I'm gagging and trying just as hard to suck in air as I am willing more of her into me. I need more of her inside me. Obligingly, she adds another finger and takes me over and over again and won't stop after I've come once, twice, ten times. I lose count as I go out of my mind because she won't fucking stop, won't give me a chance to catch my breath, and I no longer care if I ever breathe again. She fucks me like she's furious at the universe for having kept us apart so long and she has to make up for all those lost nights of passion and sweat, the days of lust and pure bliss. We've had decades in this lifetime—centuries together in those past—still, any time apart feels like the fates tormenting us. I scream and writhe and cry out until I have no voice left.

It is only later. Much later. Quite a while after she's fucked me into oblivion that she doubles back, retraces her steps, straps on her cock and takes her time. Slowly. So excruciatingly slow. She teases me to a point of so much more pain than her more violent actions could ever cause. I can't stand it and it's only then that the tears start to rise for me, the first one welling up in the corner of my eye. I feel it catch in my throat as she pushes into me such that I can feel her going on forever. Do they even make cocks long enough that you can enter someone for days before hitting a wall and then withdraw for the following week? That is how long it takes her to complete just one thrust. And the intimacy of it all is terrifying. Something that, despite the ease and comfort of our everyday, I've never gotten used to. There were precious few before her, yet none ever delivered like this. This is it for me. It always has been.

Just when I think it'll never end, she pulls out of me completely. She needs more of her inside me. So she smears thick lube across her entire hand, up over the knuckles, all the way to her wrist. I gasp in anticipation. I haven't been fucked in a month and don't think I can take that much. But she proves me wrong. Of course I can, four fingers sliding inside me with ease—sometimes she knows my body better than I do—and it's only a matter of seconds before she curves in her thumb and my pussy swallows her fist whole. Surprisingly quiet, I'd have expected screams to be tearing through my vocal cords by now. Instead my diaphragm drops and I feel another opening up from deep inside. My rib cage expands and the back of my throat dilates as I wish it would when I deep-throat her cock. With the sharp twist of her wrist, she forces me to hit a pitch so high it's barely audible and I shudder as the orgasm echoes throughout my entire body. I feel a sound escape my chest, originating from lower still. The purest note that ever graced my lips, it sails right past them and floats up in the air. I imagine an opera singer hitting her highest note.

Every time I go in for her well-guarded pleasure, I'm careful. Something about this dance makes it feel like the first time despite being territory well trod. I read every last cue her body is putting off, initiating as though it's about me. It isn't. It's about her. And us. But I'm good at making it seem like it's about me, at burrowing down to somewhere sacred. I straddle her leg, grind my wetness against her thick thigh, moan in her ear at how good she's making me feel. As my tongue searches out her tragus piercing, she groans, and I can feel the reverberations making their way through her body. Knowing how erogenous this spot is—this tiny little flap on the inside of her ear—knowing just what to do with it is quite the powerful blessing indeed. There are so many blessings to having known a body through this many moons. I take the ring between my teeth and tug, gently at first, and gradually work my way up to the point where it's going to rip out of either my teeth or her ear. One of my favorite ways to get her going. And one of hers.

Getting to fuck her is a precious gift and I honor it, giving this intimate interaction the reverence it deserves. Her desire is all tangled up in mine and it's impossible to separate the two—it would feel too unnatural, too painful to do so. So I treat it as one. Make it about how she's getting me off while I'm edging my way in. Down to the place inside her that calls for me and has been heavily secured, sentry-protected for centuries.

I move my hips in a tight figure eight and grind harder against her thigh, my juices gushing down her leg. She begins to grunt, "Oh, god..." but before she's even made it to the second word, I'm pressing my hip into her sex, and then she's adding a few extra syllables to a monosyllabic word, elongating the moan buried mid-oh while I draw out her pleasure. I wrap my mouth around her tit. My tongue delighting in how its efforts are immediately rewarded by the feel of her nipple tightening, beginning to rise, pleading for more. I graze my teeth against it, reaching over to pinch and slightly twist the other one, bite down and then release. I bring my free hand to my lips and slip two fingers into my mouth—her eyes widening, she can't help but salivate. A slow, deliberate extraction, they glisten prettily with my spit in the low light. I lower them between her thighs, as I watch her face for clues. Her eyes brim with a love so deep and true. Easing my fingers into her ass first, I work them against her G-spot until she's wordlessly begging me to slide into her cunt.

I delve in heartfirst, straight down to a deep, well-hidden place. It scares her to no end, yet she's always granted me access. I know even before her tears surface that I have dug right down to her inner aquifer. I reached the seemingly unattainable place inside her and saturated it with love and all things beautiful, filling her in ways she hadn't dared to think possible in her youth, making it known in the deepest part of her that I treasure and adore all of her. Her entire, complex, multilayered gorgeous self; her magnificently powerful presence; her exquisitely soft underbelly. No matter what the world has ever told her in the past, I deliver the message that she is strong and sweet and capable and good. And right. So very, *very* right. In all of who she is, in everything she does and says, in exactly how she makes her way through the world. She is praiseworthy and perfect. Which is not to say she is unflawed. There have been plenty of fights about the toothpaste and how she wasn't there for me during some rough times. But right now, in this very moment, I am loving her so completely, flaws and all. Every last drop of her, prized and celebrated.

I am her safe haven. Something about her since day one sparked my overwhelming need to protect her. She's learned that she can just stay here, nestled deep inside me. I squeeze my thighs together hard, holding her there tightly, letting her fill me. I protect her from the harshness of the outside world, wrapping myself around her and not letting go. This is the place where she can cry and feel safe and cherished and overcome by it all and she can just be.

When the deluge gives way to drizzle and then dries into traces of salt on her cheeks, she reaches down and runs her fingers between my lips. "So. Fucking. Wet." Just the feel of what she's done to me on a physical, primal level imbues a shared levitation. We float somewhere above this tangible world; together we vibrate internally on a higher plane. Grinding against each other with a deep-seated fury, it amplifies our envy of that other world where our souls are completely intertwined, entangled, melded together without seams. Our bodies are so limited in that regard—no matter how thoroughly she opens herself to me and I to her, there's only so much beyond fingers, fists, tongues that we can corporally accommodate.

We writhe against one another with increasing violence, knowing we are stretched to our physical limits by each other's fists. We tear into each other with hopes of the impossible, wanting to emulate the amaranthine nature of the other plane, where all of her is consumed by my sex, my soul. And her fervor devours me. A boundless existence, anything is possible, no laws of space or time. Our combined ardor set ablaze, we are a mess of twisted limbs, cum- and sweat-drenched flesh, grasping to get a better hold, pushing into each other with desperation. Floating above our selves in a heightened awareness—all our somatic senses piqued and concurrently connected to both places. Deeply rooted in our bodies while pushing them to extreme edges of earthly passions. Experiencing the ethereal desires where everything within and beyond our imaginations is granted. A chaotic whirlwind of *ohhhs* and *yeses* and begging and panting swirls around us as the flood gates give way to our frenzied lust and I'm clamping down on her fiercely, she's shuddering against me, we're crying out into the heavens, drowning in each other.

She takes me there.

DARRELL

Jay Lawrence

I have a wonderfully secluded little garden at my house by the sea. In the winter, when the fog rolls in from the bay, it sleeps, a neatly walled twilight zone of barren stick-like plants and covered patio furniture. In the summer, however, my garden comes into its own, rapidly swelling to a dazzling crescendo of fruit and flowers. I love bright colors and unusual, flamboyant plants. An ascending chorus line of terra-cotta pots edges the steps up to my kitchen door, containing a nursery of kiwi fruit, kumquats and hibiscus.

Last August, a former lover decided to pay me a surprise call. As always, during the warmer months, I had installed myself and my laptop at the little table on the slightly uneven red brick square that serves as my patio. I was trying to summon the Muse, who appeared to be taking a day off, when a familiar voice called from beyond the wrought iron gate.

"Hey there!"

"Why, hello, Darrell! Where on earth did *you* spring from? Come on in."

The gate creaked softly as Darrell entered and I noticed that she carried a well-stuffed holdall. Questions regarding the state of play of her long-term relationship came to mind but were dismissed in favor of a welcoming hug and kiss.

"You look tired, darling. Let me make you some tea."

Darrell sank into a chair and smiled up at me, all bright blue eyes and a halo of soft golden hair. She looked like an angel.

"I've left Karen. It's for the best."

"I'm so sorry. Oh dear, I don't really know what to say."

Darrell's expression was as enigmatic as the Mona Lisa's.

"Then don't say anything at all! Some things simply aren't meant to be. I don't suppose you have any of that glorious apricot tea left?"

Ah, Darrell, ever the little pragmatist. Like a cat, she'd always fall on her feet. I watched my girl kick off her sandals and stretch out in the dappled, sun-splashed light of the patio. Two years before, I had lost Darrell to Karen, a tall, brusque redhead with an architect's business in Manhattan. I wasn't bitter. It was hard to bear a grudge against someone like Darrell.

In my tiny yellow kitchen with shells arranged upon the window ledge, I boiled water and searched for the special fruity tea. There was just enough left to make a small pot for two and I recalled the origins of the heady brew, an old-fashioned store in Greenwich Village. Darrell had worn a great big scarf to keep out the November chill, looking every inch the student she was. Yellowed maple leaves were thick on the ground as I kissed her, tracing her cold cheeks with my worshipful hands.

"Here we are, Daz."

The old endearment slipped so easily from my lips as I set a tray down upon the garden table. I'd used a clear glass teapot and the hot liquid within glowed like the purest amber. I noticed that Darrell's dress had somehow risen above her lovely knees, revealing a glorious sweep of gleaming suntanned leg. She grinned at me like a mischievous child and I suddenly realized that I could forgive her anything. Half-amused, part annoyed and just plain happy to see the girl, I poured the fragrant tea into porcelain cups.

"You always did have wonderful taste, Suzy. I envy you."

That made me laugh out loud. There was my gorgeous girl, veritably glittering in the afternoon sun, humbly admiring my fine but mismatched thrift-store china. She shifted slightly in her chair, crossing her legs and magically revealing an extra inch or two of thigh. Terminally artful and absolutely adorable.

"Are those peaches, Suze? They look marvelous!"

I followed Darrell's gaze to the heavily laden tree, which I had carefully espaliered against the south-facing wall of my little sanctuary. A multitude of blushing downy globes had rewarded my care and I had been planning a lengthy canning session that very evening. Peaches are my favorite fruit, and there's nothing can brighten a dark winter's day more than a spoonful of luscious gold from my well-stocked pantry.

The grass felt cool and moist beneath my feet as I padded across the lawn and selected the finest, ripest fruit for my impromptu guest.

"You don't get this in the city."

I thought of Karen's industrial-chic loft, all white empty space and Bauhaus chairs, like living in some monochromatic Lego set. Karen herself, lean and taut with Pilates, poles apart from my homely charms. I placed the peach in Darrell's lap, an offering to the goddess. She looked down and smiled.

"You're so sweet. Would you peel it for me, please? I'm so hopeless, I always get in a terrible mess."

"Of course."

I returned to the kitchen to fetch a knife and, as an afterthought, a bright paper napkin with a pattern of sunflowers. Glancing through the window as I rummaged in a cluttered drawer, I spotted my friend surreptitiously unbuttoning the bodice of her dress. Suddenly my mouth was dry, as if every last drop of moisture had rushed to the warm oasis between my legs.

Well, my beloved, you certainly didn't waste any time. And you know I'm caught just like a fish on your hook.

Conflicting emotions surged through me as I stood, transfixed, watching Darrell remove her dress. Did she sense that she had a captive audience of one? It was an unself-conscious striptease. A ray of sunlight caressed her breasts as she unhooked her bra, and my pussy responded with a soft yet insistent fluttering sensation. Butterflies of desire. Slowly, as if determined to maintain at least a semblance of dignity, I descended to the patio, clasping the knife and napkin in moist hands. My heart was beating like a drum.

Darrell was stretched out on the grass like a big calico cat. I almost expected her to purr expectantly as I sat down beside her with my votive offering. I couldn't help smiling as I swiftly peeled and sliced the velvety fruit. Only Daz would have the nerve, the sheer insouciance to arrive without warning, requesting her special tea, asking me to prepare her peach as if nothing had changed since that Greenwich November and Karen the architect didn't exist. I felt as if I should be building some kind of emotional wall but, dammit, I just wanted the girl. Wanted her and loved her too.

"What *am* I going to do with you?"

"You could start by kissing me."

Darrell giggled and opened her arms. I felt a kind of inner rush, like being enveloped by a warm tide. I just wanted to dive on into her welcoming embrace. I knew I was being used, but

I didn't care. I kissed the girl. Her lips tasted sweet and faintly sticky, as if she'd been eating candy on her journey. The previous months melted away as we reconnected, lost time dissolving as surely as the honey in our tea. Finally, we came up for air, both breathing hard. I looked down at Darrell's face. Her eyes were closed; a faint smile played upon her lips and her cheeks were flushed. I admired her beautiful breasts, which were quite small but ultra-firm, their tips upturned. Pert and perky tits. I had always lavished attention on Darrell's breasts.

The sun felt heavy on my back as I knelt between my lover's parted thighs and dipped my hot tea-sweet mouth to suck upon her small pink nipples. They felt like firm jellied candies against my massaging tongue. The butterflies returned, beating their pleasuring wings deep within my syrupy pussy. I took a slice of juicy peach and placed it against my lover's slightly parted lips, simultaneously caressing her silky inner thigh. Darrell sighed, a long, sibilant sound like the sea rushing up the gravel beach to greet the dunes. Slowly, as if she knew it would drive me wild, she drew the dripping wedge of fruit into her mouth and held it there.

"Why don't you feed me, Daz?"

Her eyes half opened, glittering dreamy slits in her sun-kissed face. I counted the tiny freckles on her sweet snub nose as she squeezed the slice of peach out through her plump and sticky lips. A nub of orange-pink flesh emerged from her mouth, so resembling a swollen clitoris that I began to flick the fruit with my tongue. The ripe fruit slid down my throat and I swallowed greedily as my hand instinctively strayed to the soaking place between my legs. My thin panties were drenched and I shivered as Darrell's cool fingers reached up to ease them over my hips and down my thighs. Swiftly, I wriggled out of my sundress and tossed it onto the grass. Suddenly, it was as if we couldn't stand to have the slightest wisp of fabric between our bodies. Almost roughly, I nipped at her skimpy panties with my teeth, dragging them down to reveal her perfumed velvety pussy.

"You look just like a peach!"

It was true. I'd always thought Darrell had the most beautiful pussy. She had a lovely plump Mound of Venus, which was usually either shaved smooth or trimmed to leave but a fine dusting of reddish gold, a mere bloom of soft curly hair. Her labia were small but perfectly formed. She was, indeed, the most tempting fruit of all, as she lay like some magnificent windfall beneath the whispering branches of my tiny orchard. The afternoon sun seemed to caress my naked back as I slipped on top of my lover in a sixty-nine. My lips found her clit and I began to lap up her musky juice, tracing the satiny contours of her inner curves with my searching tongue.

"Eat me, Daz!"

Almost tentatively, Darrell's mouth captured my own ripe to bursting fruit. I could take no more than a few brief moments of her intense wet heat before crying out with my first orgasm. As soon as the waves subsided, I placed my mouth over her solid, shiny clit and sucked like a five-year-old enjoying a lollipop. I remembered Darrell. She was the kind of girl who took a lot of stimulation. I'd long suspected that Karen spanked her, taking full advantage of her slight passivity, but ours was a meeting of equals. I licked and sucked and flicked the tiny female cock, savoring the smooth silk of her fresh clean flesh, the salty sugar of her copious juice. Darrell aroused slowly but steadily, as if her body chose to climb a long, steep plateau and make brief ecstasy last forever. Her hands felt warm, sometimes playing with my hair, sometimes pressing softly on my back, guiding me gently, encouraging me to stay the course. I could sense her orgasm rise, swell, grow, from a well hidden seed in the depths of her love-nest to a full, ripe, bursting, juice-filled crescendo. As she almost reached her peak, she began to thrash around from side to side, as if to come was just too intense, too much for her body to bear. She took her time but when she came it was explosive.

"Oh, fuck me! Oh, please fuck me!"

I kept my mouth on her clit, never missing a beat, but slipped the tip of one finger inside her ass. Darrell's whole body seemed to rise; she writhed like an ivory serpent on the grass.

"Oh no, oh no, oh no, oh no..."

I remembered her pleading, as if she almost had to fight the relentless onslaught of her orgasm. Nobody came like Darrell came. It was all I could do to hold on to her as she ground her shaking hips against my face. I was coated in her juice from forehead to chin. Finally, joyfully, her body imploded beneath my tongue and she screamed, wailed, moaned a veritable Greek chorus accompanying a climax that could waken the dead.

"Oh god, oh my darling..."

It took her a while to subside, to slowly come back down to earth, so I gently dismounted and brought her her tepid tea, patiently waiting for my lover to recover. From time to time she shuddered with little aftershocks, as if she had been plugged into a powerful electrical source and now had to shed the current amp by amp. Suddenly I felt overwhelmingly protective.

"You're precious to me, you know."

Darrell looked up at me, her bright gaze a hybrid of gratitude and triumph. She made a slight face as she sipped the half-cold apricot tea.

"You're so sweet, Suze! There's so much I have to tell you."

"There's plenty of time. No hurry. I'm not going anywhere."

My lover smiled ruefully, but truthfully, I hadn't meant to

imply anything. I wouldn't be going anywhere because permanence is my style. I'm a patient sort. I understand that the seasons turn and birds fly south in winter, only to return when the weather is fine. I love the slow, sensual rhythm of my garden. Sometimes it sleeps, sometimes it sings with a riot of color. If I tend it, it rewards me with baskets full of fruit. Darrell is a butterfly. She lives completely in the present, without regret. I know I can never possess her, I can only seize the day. And so, that drowsy August afternoon, I got her to help me with my peach canning. I decided to store up sweet fruit and memories to ward off future chill. My lover comes and goes. Sometimes, months pass and all I have is a postcard on my fridge, stamped in Albuquerque or Spokane. I deal with it. Summer can't last forever, but it always returns.

COOLING DOWN, HEATING UP

Dena Hankins

I use the ribbed cotton of my tank top to dry the skin under my tits. A bra would soak up some of the sweat, but I can't bear one thread more than the top and my underwear. I'm sitting on the floor, leaning against the fieldstone fireplace in our 180-year-old farmhouse. Never thought the fireplace would be the coolest spot in the house.

The fan squeaks a bit, way up in the high ceiling. I'll have to fix that when it's not a million degrees. The blades pour humid air over me like a warm river.

Hennie's flushed, lying flat on her back in a cotton slip she made herself. It's got thin lines of lace, top and bottom, and she scratches at her thigh where the lace tickles. She wiggles within reach, hunting a cooler spot on the wooden floor, and I poke her hip with my big toe. She groans. "I love you, sweetheart. Don't touch me."

I laugh.

The hills outside Chapel Hill, North Carolina, sport more

than one lovely old house. Ours has little in the way of grounds—the fields had been sold long before we came around. We've owned it three years now, moved in on our eighth anniversary. Still getting bruised and blistered working on it, but that's just part of owning an old home. Our bedroom is straight out of the nineteenth century, except we made the dressing room into a bathroom. We updated the kitchen but left the cupboards. The old plumbing complains and we replace what we have to.

Mostly, we restore what we can and live without plenty. Like air-conditioning.

"Hennie, I think it's time."

My lover smiles without opening her eyes. "Gettin' itchy?"

"Mmm-hmm."

Hennie sits up with a whoosh and blinks like she's light-headed. Her slip's wet where she was lying on it. Her tits are bare under the thin cotton and her nipples are soft, nearly flat in the heat. "Want to make reservations or pack?"

I lever myself to my feet and wish I hadn't. "I'll pack."

Hennie laughs. "You're sweet, but I was joking. Get on the computer and I'll put together an overnight bag."

I lean over and give Hennie my hand. We both groan at the sticky feeling as I pull her upright. Pressing my lips to hers without touching anywhere else, I mumble against her mouth, "You're the one for me."

"I'd better be." Her grumpy tone makes me smile and she pulls away. Slogging through the dank air, she heads up the stairs to our bedroom on the second floor. Her voice fades as she gripes, "I still say we should have a summer bedroom downstairs. We can put a bed in the piano parlor and..."

My face settles into the expression Hennie calls "mulish." I consider that an insult and refuse to cop to it. I love our bedroom and won't give it up for anything. A smile breaks through. Actually, I will give it up tonight for that most modern of conveniences.

We're driving away less than an hour later and pull up to the chain motel a half hour after that. After checking in, we drive around the back and park in front of the door to our room for the night.

Hennie slides the key card into the reader and shoves against the seal made by the weather stripping. She gasps and calls out, "It's already cold in here!" The delight in her voice is worth the sixty dollars we just dropped.

Holding the bag, I lock the car doors and follow her into the room. The temperature drops at the door and I shiver hard. Hennie's inspecting the room—opening drawers, checking out the bathroom. Reminds me of a dog sniffing new territory when she does that, though I'd never make the mistake of saying so. She starts the shower and yells, "Good pressure."

The shower doesn't stop. She must have decided to jump right in. Would she want something to wear afterward? I'll probably ruin a surprise if I open the bag, so I decide against getting clothes out for her. Maybe we won't wear anything until it's time to check out.

Water hits the wall and the shower curtain, the sound modulating as she moves. I picture her turning under the spray, cupping her hands and letting the cool water overflow down her chest.

I can't stay all sticky while she's getting so clean.

Down with my shorts, off with my underwear. The tank top droops, heavy with my sweat, and the chilling fabric draws another shiver from me as I pull it over my head. Damn. The cold is almost as uncomfortable as the heat.

In the cold, though, we can get close.

I push open the door to the little bathroom and it stops

against the shower/tub combo. Hennie's slip is limp on the floor and I catch my first sight of her in the vanity mirror across from the shower.

Her deep curves make my insides tighten. Through the translucent plastic shower curtain, she has the mysterious proportions of a goddess. Her heavy hips and solid thighs taper to strong calves and small feet, while above...ah, above.

Hennie's breasts curve away from her ribs, lower than they were when we first stripped for one another. We attacked each other that night with the lights out. Not for shyness, but because we were in such a hurry that we forgot to turn them on.

Since then, Hennie has put on thirty, maybe forty pounds. Her breasts are heavier, her ass more padded. Her waist still has that delicious curve and her face barely shows a difference, but she looks so much more womanly to me. As a girl, she charmed me. Now I am devoted to the woman she's become.

Physically, I've always been a tit woman. I love a shapely ass, but it's big, soft tits that catch my attention when I'm supposed to be driving. When I'm shopping for groceries. When I'm ordering a meal. I love large, pillowy breasts.

Hennie's were unreal when we met—high and too firm to make deep cleavage. In my opinion, they've gotten better. They've softened, gained a deeper under-curve and, in the right bra, they push together for some jaw-dropping cleavage. It's not just me—everyone notices.

"Are you coming in or are you going to stare all night?"

I grin. "I'm doing more than staring tonight. It's been two weeks since it's been cool enough to lick your pussy, let alone fuck you." I push the curtain back and our eyes meet. "How's the shower?"

My pussy thumps when she steps sideways, letting the water sluice over her tits. "Invigorating."

"Just what I wanted to hear."

"Come on in, then."

The sultry look she gives me is hotter than the weather outside our motel room. I step over the lip of the tub and take the motel soap from her hands. She turns away while I build up a good froth. Reaching out, I slick my hands across her shoulders and sigh.

My libido doesn't disappear, but the familiar happiness of touching Hennie—scratching her back lightly, gripping the muscles of her shoulders and squeezing them in my hands—this overwhelms my lust with tenderness. We have time to be fierce with one another. First I just want to get close.

Hennie hums and tips her head back when I slide up behind her. Shower spray wets my front and I bring my tits and belly up against her soapy back. I slide my arms around her waist and hold her close.

My love likes to pretend that I am the horndog in the relationship, but she's the one who starts sliding her ass on my thighs. She's the one who lifts my hands to cup her tits and grabs the back of my neck over her shoulder. She acts like I'm the one who gets itchy and needy, but Hennie's desire burns and demands, where mine tends to glow. If I'm an ocean swell, she's that wave from *The Perfect Storm.*

"I love you," I breathe in her ear. I nibble the outer curve and suck her earlobe between my teeth. Moments like this, I'm glad I'm taller than she is. I can see her tits mounded in my palms while I run my teeth down the muscle in her neck. The taste of cheap soap makes my nose wrinkle and I let the shower rinse my mouth.

I focus on her nipples. Hennie says they're not very sensitive, but to me, they're perfect. She can take a lot of sensation. I like tugging on them hard, twisting them, gnawing and sucking. It sends me over the edge to have them in my mouth, and some of our strangest sex positions have resulted from my desire for Hennie's tits.

She asked me once what I'd do if she got breast cancer and had them chopped off. I teared up and she got pissed before I could pull it together. I wasn't crying over some damn breast tissue, though. I freak out when she gets a splinter. I don't know how I'd handle a major illness like cancer. Can't stand to think about it. I hope we age well and die together in our sleep.

Hennie must feel my change of mood, me thinking about sickness and old age, because she turns in my arms and hugs me tight. She slides a hand into my spiky hair and pulls my head down to her shoulder. I squeeze her and marvel at the complicated swell of emotion—desperate love, warm affection, a hint of future sadness born of my need for her. Under all that, though, the slippery body of my lover stokes my lust.

"Finish your shower, but don't come out until you holler." Hennie gives the order, knowing I'll bristle at her tone and get excited at the same time. She turns around under the spray for a final rinse and steps out.

I soap up and let the water run over me, warm water over cool skin. Been taking cold showers for a couple months, and a warm shower is a strange treat. Cold feels good, don't mistake me, but it don't relax a body.

I scrub my body dry—Hennie tells me to pat, but I like the scratching—and tug the locks over my eyebrows into a disarray that I hope is sexy.

"Ready for me, honey?" I'm turning the doorknob as I yell.

"Come and get it," my lover growls.

I step out of the bathroom and suck in a breath. My turn, is it?

Hennie stands in front of the heavy drapes, stroking the dark blue dildo in her harness. The straps follow the curve of her hips. Her hair curls around the edges of the backing pad and her belly swells gently above. The dildo is long and not very wide. I raise an eyebrow and meet her challenging look. "It's been a while," I say, by way of a warning.

"I'm feeling patient. It's not the only dildo I brought, though."

We have a few dildos we use in our harnesses. She's wearing the one we use for butt-play, and I turn my attention to my body. Clenching my sphincters and releasing them, I feel good—clean and clear, warming up to the idea of getting fucked. It's not my usual role, but Hennie's excited and that decides me.

"Let's see how it goes."

Hennie sends me her sly "got what I wanted" smile. We meet at the foot of the bed and push close, kissing deeply and squeezing the dildo between our bellies. I press the sides of her breasts with my upper arms while stroking my hands along the waist strap of the harness.

Hennie strokes my neck and shoulders, pressing her thumbs along my collarbones. I pull away and she gives me a little push so I land on the bed, on top of the damp towel she laid out from her shower. I catch myself, half-reclined with my hands braced on the bed behind me, and Hennie attacks.

My elbows fold under her weight and my breathing stops altogether with her nipple in my mouth. She thrusts the dildo against my belly, straddling me, giving me the writhing armful that gets me hot. She knows the buttons and she's pushing them all as though we're going for a quickie in a park. I reach down, but the bulk of her gorgeous ass prevents me from finding her cunt from behind.

With a whimper—the least butch sound I make—I burrow my hand between our bodies and past the dildo and harness.

Slippery, swollen and hot. My love makes fists and pounds them on the bed, determined that I will not distract her, determined not to let me flip her so that she gets fucked first. She pushes her ass upward, out of my reach, and pulls her nipple out of my mouth.

"Not this time," she says, looking like an angry schoolmarm. "You fucking lie there."

I bump my hips up at her. Hennie falls back on top of me and laughs. She never does stay mad for long. She scoots down and parts my legs. The dildo bumps against my cunt and I squirm again. She puts a hand on my chest for stability and uses the other to open me up. The dildo slides a tiny ways into my cunt. I'm wet enough to slick that silicone up just fine.

Miniature thrusts and a thumb on my clit hood frustrate me, but I know she's doing it for my own good. Only way to put me into the zone is to tease me. I can come, no problem, but it's usually minor muscle spasms. For the full-body clench and release, I have to get to a much higher level of need.

Hennie's looking at my cheeks, watching me lick my lips. She presses down on my rib cage and watches my nipples harden. The calculating way she manipulates my clit, rubbing above and to each side without touching it, makes me stretch my arms up and grab for the headboard.

But we're not in our bed. My fingers scrabble against veneer and I settle for a pillow, grabbing it between my hands and wishing I had something to pull against.

Hennie is satisfied that I'm with her. She hates it when I let her fuck me, but there's no connection. She says I may as well just masturbate when I'm like that, and she's not wrong. Right now, though, it's Hennie's touch and Hennie's plan that's ratcheting my body tighter and tighter.

She slides her knees up, one at a time, shoving my legs wide and draping them over her thighs. Kneeling, she leaves the dildo in my cunt, where it teases me with hints of pleasure without being wide enough to stretch me the way I love. She gloves one hand, lubes up both, and slides the gloved one below the dildo.

Her fingers slip over the tiny folds around my asshole and dance around the ring of muscle holding it closed. Slipping in the lube, her fingers press and massage that ring until I feel it happen. I start to open up.

Meeting my eyes, she dallies until I exhale. Her teasing thumb presses my clit finally and then, as I arch up into that touch, she slips her index finger inside my ass. I can't help the clench that follows. It's not a rejection. It's a plea to stay.

Gently rubbing me all around, she focuses on easing my tightness. I do my best to help out with deep breathing, but Hennie doesn't want me too relaxed. She keeps stroking my clit, but only in ways that don't, won't get me off. Eventually, my eyes slide shut and my hips start to wander.

That's the moment Hennie's been waiting for. When I move into hungry receptivity, she pulls the dildo from my cunt and slides it a tiny bit into my ass. The hand on my clit goes still and then her palm presses against it, giving me something to rub on without distracting me from the deep give of my ass opening to her. Took a lot of fucking for her to pinpoint the moment when the clit stimulation needed to stop, but she nailed it this time.

I love this moment. I can feel muscles slacken inside my body, muscles I'm not aware of on a day-to-day basis. She slides in and my insides rearrange to accommodate her. Fresh lube cools the dildo and is warmed by friction. When she stops pressing, I open my eyes.

"It's working." She presses harder against my clit as she speaks.

"Oh, yeah."

I lie on my back in an unfamiliar room, with an over-bleached motel towel under my impaled ass and goose bumps covering my body. The strangeness of our surroundings excite me, but not as much as the woman between my legs. Hennie looks abstracted, focused on the feedback she gets from the hand wrapped around the dildo. Her hips are still and she manipulates the dildo in tiny circles with her hand, watching my ass tighten and soften in response. Her intense attention is all for my body, and my body gives her what she wants.

"I think you're ready." Hennie looks up into my face, checking in.

I nod, opening my mouth to agree. A moan escapes when she pulls the dildo from my ass. Hungry to get it back, I scramble to turn over and present my ass, high and ready for her.

She makes me wait. She drifts up close behind me and slides her knees between my thighs. She lays the dildo's length between my cheeks and thrusts slowly, the slick silicone rubbing against the hot softness of my asshole. A cool deluge strikes and I flinch. Hennie laughs and rubs the lube around my asshole with the dildo, then angles it down for me.

I back down on it, gobbling it up, filling myself up and then slowing down so I can take more. It's a very long dildo and, in this position, Hennie can get close enough to give me every inch. I thrust my ass onto it a bit at a time, moaning at the depth of my penetration.

When I get all the way down on it, I push against Hennie's thighs with mine and press my asscheeks into her hips. Shaking and jerking, so close to coming, I reach for my clit but she says, "No, not yet."

I almost sob, but she starts thrusting and my attention turns. Slide and slap, and she pushes her weight into my ass. She wants me to brace so I won't slide across the bed. On my knees with my ass high and my shoulders low, I grip the bedspread in hopes it'll keep me in position.

We're both fucking now, slamming into each other hard and bouncing back, just to slam together again. It's not fast, but it's relentless and we keep it up until my grip fails and I slide forward. Hennie grabs my hips then and pulls my ass into her. I reach down for my clit and she doesn't stop me. That turns me on even more, because it means she knows how worked up I am.

My mind is clouded, dislocated. I am thinking with my gut. My clit is enormous and so is Hennie's dildo in my ass. I reach inside my cunt to feel it move. The end strokes my fingers through the thin tissue that separates one hole from the other and I have my face and chest pressed into the bed with both hands on my cunt now. Hennie is chanting, "Come for me, baby. Come for me." I'm rubbing my clit and filling my cunt. Hennie is fucking my ass so smoothly that in and out feel the same and the orgasm builds from the deepest part of me that she touches, disintegrating my flesh and replacing it with pure energy.

When the pulses slow and subside, my body re-forms around the sensation of Hennie pulling her dildo from my ass. She slips to the side, running one hand down my back, then removes the harness. While I'm still dazed, reeling from being discorporate with pleasure, Hennie turns me over.

I flop over gladly, my ass still pulsing, and take a deep breath. Good thing, too, because Hennie's pussy covers my mouth, lips held open by her slick fingers. The scent and texture of her becomes part of my lingering orgasm and I lap at her slowly. Hennie is too far gone for that, though, and she shoves her clit at my tongue.

I'm buried and helpless under her, but she only needs me to keep my tongue curled and my lips pursed. She fucks me again, this time with her clit in my mouth, climbing so quickly to orgasm that she must have been close when I came. She grabs the fake headboard in front of her and the bed pounds the wall from her jagged thrusts until she keens, a high, thin sound that means it's holding off, that the orgasm she's chasing is just beyond her reach. I add a flick of my tongue to the end of her movement and she convulses above me, belly quaking and tits shivering.

By the time her cries have lowered in pitch, I have my wits about me again. I love this woman and she has given me so much. When she gets off me, still moaning, I slip off the bed and grab the bag.

Sure enough, she also packed my harness and the fat dildo she loves so much. I strap it on. She's done all the work so far, but now I'm ready to break a sweat. Why not? We've got air-conditioning.

PHONE CALL AWAY

Derek Shannon

Sophie checked the clock for the hundredth time, trying to keep herself busy with pointless dusting around the bedroom, rearranging pictures and souvenirs and books on the shelves, her heart racing, her mouth dry. She couldn't stop herself, and for a moment considered going to the loo but settled for stopping at her chest of drawers and staring at the photo taking center place. There she was, wearing that hideous pink-and purple-striped jumper like she was a middle-aged lesbian Roald Dahl character, with a big stupid grin on her face and those stupid round Harry Potter glasses she thankfully got rid of two months ago...

But she didn't keep the photo because of herself.

Beside her, clad in her desert camouflage uniform and grinning equally stupidly, Sergeant Keisha Achebe stood almost a head taller, a coffee-skinned contrast to Sophie's lighter Nordic features, a beauty who took Sophie's heart with her when she shipped away to the other side of the world.

It hadn't been easy for Sophie, though she never showed her anxiety to her family or friends, some of whom never quite got past the idea that their precious little Sophie was gay—and Sophie was pushing into her thirties. More than one night, after watching the news, Sophie would find herself in bed, crying, tugging at her hair so hard she feared she'd find blond locks in her fist in the morning. More than one night, Sophie would curse Keisha for joining the army, even if Keisha insisted in every letter and phone call that she was far away from the fighting over there. Sophie knew better—or at least, the dark paranoid corners of her knew better.

Wasn't it six o'clock yet?

She'd forgone eating after getting out of work, but now her stomach was growling beneath her tight black T-shirt. Perhaps she could go have a quick snack before—

The Bluetooth phone receiver in her ear chirped. Her heart raced, but she stayed in control, remembering the time she practically squealed down the line at what turned out to be a cold caller from Mumbai. "Hello?"

"Sophie Muffin?"

She grinned at the voice. "Key! Tell me you're okay, nothing's wrong, you're all still in one piece!"

A familiar sigh preceded the reply. "I'm okay, nothing's wrong and yes, I'm all still in one piece. I work in the fucking kitchens, Soph. The only shell fragments I encounter are from eggs."

Sophie danced around the bedroom like she'd been given a booster shot of bliss. It was Keisha, it was Keisha, it was lovely Keisha in her ear! "I'm gonna keep asking until you're back here, you know."

"I know." A pause, and then, "I miss you, Sophie Muffin."

Sophie forced herself to sit down on the bed. "I miss you too." The tears were welling up already, and she breathed hard to stem the flow. Keisha didn't have too much time for the call, and Sophie was determined not to waste it. "Hey, guess who's getting hitched? Jane and Holly!"

"What, those two? Bollocks. Holly will be back at the Castor in a week for fresh pussy."

"You're such a cynic."

"No, I'm realistic. The girl hits on anything with a vagina."

"And you know this, how?"

Another pause. "A girl can tell."

"Has she tried it on you?"

"Mmm...maybe."

Sophie pursed her lips. "I was gonna buy them a toaster! Now I'll smack her in the mouth the next time I see her."

Keisha laughed that glorious laugh of hers.

"I'll do it." Sophie grinned despite herself. "Don't you believe me?"

"I believe you're about as threatening as Winnie the Pooh."

"Bitch. You're probably right."

"Of course I'm right. I know you better than anyone else."

Sophie smiled. "Yes. You do. Oh, and I'm thinking of getting us a new bed."

"Fuck, I would hope so. The springs on my side are noisier than a jackhammer."

Sophie laughed. "And on mine."

"Didn't we end up fucking at the foot just so not to disturb the neighbors?"

She touched the lavender quilt cover, memories flooding back of that time: their naked flesh touching, lips tasting, fingers moving and delving and pleasing, taking each other to sublime heights. She looked up at the cracked, plastered ceiling she'd stared up at so many times. "Do you love me, Key?"

"Course I do. Fancy the hell out of you too."

"Indulge me, then. Tell me something you miss."

A pause, and then Keisha responded. "I remember the dirty late-night calls we'd make when we were still dating. Hearing you touching yourself while we talked was...you know."

She remembered and warmed to the memories of those calls. Keisha's voice took her places she'd never gone before and cemented their relationship. "'You know?' How coy. You can be dirtier than that on the phone. Or maybe you've lost your touch?"

Keisha paused. "You get my pussy throbbing, Soph. Just at the thought of you. It throbs and aches."

That was more like it. Sophie said, "Throbs and aches, huh? To do what?"

Keisha's voice was husky, heavy. "To feel your tongue slip between my pussy lips and fill me to the brim. To cling together as we fuck, long and slow and hard."

Tremors suffused her. Keisha's voice...it reached her as no other ever did, even over the phone, and it made her pussy twitch as strongly now as it had the first time she'd heard it. She settled back some more, fingertips stroking her cheek, brushing across her lips. "Are you wet now?"

"Yes."

Sophie nibbled at her finger, slipping back into a familiar game she had all but forgotten, wanting to dispel the melancholy she had been feeling. "Well, I don't know what I can do about that, with you out in that dusty country and me here..."

"I do. Touch your breasts."

She licked her lips, but still feigned modesty. "But...but that would be rude."

Keisha chuckled. "Go on, touch them. They're stunning. They need touching."

Sophie smiled and slowly cupped one breast through her

black T-shirt. She had taken off her bra as soon as she'd come home, and she cupped and caressed the weight of it, the heat of it. Goose bumps rose, as did her nipple. She gasped.

"Oh god, Soph," Keisha exclaimed breathlessly. "Does it feel good?"

She sounded as distracted, as aroused, as Sophie felt, though she knew that sitting in the car on the main road, Keisha lacked privacy. "Y-Yes, Key..."

Keisha made murmurs of approval. "Imagine me there now, my lips and tongue along your nipples, as I press you down on the bed..."

Sophie bit her lip as she continued to caress her breasts. Down below, her pussy ached for attention. "Fuck, yes."

"Good. Open your jeans."

"What? I couldn't." Sophie paused. "Could I?"

"Oh yes. Why not, girl? Think of me doing it for you. Think of how wet you're getting just thinking about it."

A wave of excitement made her shiver, and she almost fumbled with her thin leather belt and the brass tab at her waist. Her mouth kept going dry, as if all of her moisture had gone elsewhere.

"Have you done it?" Keisha asked eagerly.

"Almost," she whispered. She worked the tiny strip of clenched metal of her zipper, the tabs locked together as if in an elaborate embrace. She peeled the front of her jeans open, revealing a delta of brocaded blue lace obscuring the dark trimmed thatch of pubic hair. After a moment, she drew down her jeans until they were halfway down her thighs. "Oh god..."

"Are you all right?"

"Oh yes..." She gasped aloud, feeling the air on her legs as she sat on the edge of the bed and parted her knees. "This feels so dirty."

"It should. I'm so fucking hot for you, Soph. Touch yourself."

Without thinking she snaked her hand down over her thong, pressing down against her mound. She caressed her sex, the middle finger running along the indent in the lace made by the furrow of her pussy, feeling moistness in the fabric. "Ooh, it feels lush."

"Are you wet too?"

She felt her face burn in an incredibly delicious way. "Yes. I can feel it inside me, seeping out, down my slit."

Keisha moaned. "Soph, if I was there, I'd bury my tongue in that sweet little pussy of yours."

She peeled aside the thong, touching her pubic hair, combing through it with her fingers before reaching her hot puffy flesh, releasing her musk. The sound of her moist flesh parting slightly was almost as big a jolt as when the tip of her thumb brushed over... "Oh fuck...my clit—"

Keisha grunted again. "Oh god, Soph, I wish I was there now. I wish I was kneeling between your legs, drinking in your scent, letting my tongue glide over that clit, tease and circle around it, dipping down into your pussy...You shouldn't taste so good, Sophie..."

"My hand—my hand's in my pussy." Sophie breathed hard. "I'm soaking wet." With her thumb working at her clit, her middle finger curved downward until it slipped between her labia, found the entrance to her sex, stroked the brim, thrusting sharply, shallowly, again and again. "And your tongue is working its way deep inside me...I'm flipping over to do the same to you."

"My fingers join my tongue, diving in and out of you, pumping hard and fast." Keisha's voice had taken on an urgent monotone, as it did those many nights when she would call her like this, driving her to the edge as she masturbated shamelessly.

Sophie gasped as she fell back, her legs still hanging over the foot of the bed and parted as much as she was able, the waistband of her thong ripping as she continued to masturbate furiously. "Fuck me, Key...come on—"

"I...I feel you coming...oh god, Soph—"

Sophie called out without shame as her whole body shuddered and spasmed, and she squeezed her eyes shut to the white light that permeated her. Her mouth was dry as she gasped again, relishing the hot glow running through her. Her voice cracked when she finally spoke again. "Fuck, I needed that, Key."

"Me too."

Sophie opened her eyes. "Did you touch yourself?"

A breathless laugh was followed by, "There's this old-fashioned phone booth here, like where you'd expect Clark Kent to change into Superman. And I'm in here with my hand down my pants risking a charge of public indecency, and the next woman who uses this phone is going to be sliding off the seat."

Sophie burst out laughing, riding the crest of her climax until she settled down again and melancholy threatened to dampen her spirits. "When are you coming home?"

"Six weeks, two days. A thousand and fifty-six hours, that's all."

"It's still too long."

"I know." A pause. "I love you, Sophie Muffin. And I'm only a phone call away."

RAVENS

Rachel Randall

It's Silke's terrible idea, but it's my fault for telling her my fantasy in the first place.

The night before, with her beautiful body spread over me, her breasts rasping silk against mine, it was hard to think beyond the vivid thrill of having her. Mouth hot at my ear, she'd asked her filthy questions just to tease out my stumbling answers. When she'd reached down to stroke my clit, I'd gasped into her shoulder, "I want to have you where someone could see us."

I'd been imagining a tumble in a quiet corner of Hyde Park once the weather turned warmer. Or Silke on her knees, licking me to cream and shudders in the ladies' at our local. Instead she'd crooned, "Somewhere dangerous?" and I'd stuttered, "Yeah," because I'd have agreed to anything while she fingered me there and there and *there*. Now I'm paying the price with soaked-through knickers and a sense of events spiraling out of my control.

"Risk of arrest kills the mood," I say with a hiss.

She doesn't buy it for a moment, and I can't blame her. She knows me far too well.

"But, Becky, I have a fantasy too." Not so much what she says, as how she says it—with one hip cocked and her cheeks flushed, sophistry has never looked so appealing. Then, "You need to fuck me across Sir Walter Raleigh's desk."

"Sorry?" I say, but what I think, helpless, empowered, is that it's been two years and I'm still high in the heady throes of relationship thrall. I'll happily do just about anything she suggests... wants, demands, needs, hints, *whatever.* Oh, I'm so gloriously fucked here, as colleague and girlfriend both.

At least I'm in good company at the moment, here at the Tower of London with all the ghosts of foolish lovers past. Though I hope I won't lose my head over my lady quite so thoroughly as others have done in this haunted place.

"Get a few snaps of the room, then you can shag me against the desk of a famous explorer. I'll write a column about it."

I don't ask which part of the proceedings will get the write-up. I save my breath for last-ditch diplomacy and the phone call I'll need to make to a legal team following our arrest at one of the UK's most treasured landmarks. My hands spread wide in supplication, but I sense that the red yarn of my mittens is a red flag to her mischievous grin.

"Let's go for some spooky exterior shots," I try. "The White Tower, draped in timeless Thames mists. You know tourists love that bollocks."

She smiles at me. There's a divot in her chin I want to press with my lips before moving on to the teasing laughter creases by her eyes.

The thing is—

The thing is, we're on a job at the moment. Our latest assignment as photographer and writer, and truth be told, our freelance careers are at a more delicate point than our well-established love affair. The website wants fresh content on a tired beat. I should be taking photos of "legendary London," not flirting with disaster.

To make the point, I turn my back on her to lift my Nikon. I frame an arty shot of cobblestones and bright blue doors, but I can't quite keep my hands steady as excitement trembles through me. Lowering the camera in defeat, I say, "You do realize it's very likely not his *actual* desk, right?"

"A historical replica will do," she concedes in her perfect English, "but will need a strong effort from you."

Glancing across the courtyard finds me no reprieve. The ravens, the Tower's most famous residents, are scattered across a manicured square of lawn. They're watching me, all beady eyes and sharp beaks and utterly alien dispassion. Such a contrast to the way my girl watches, smug happiness a corona around her.

It's a terrible idea. Yet the same arousal that flushes her cheeks is a warm knot in my chest.

Silke goes to court the Yeomen Warders waiting by the gate. Her robin's-egg coat is a pretty contrast to their scarlet-and-black-skirted solemnity, and her blond hair plays peek-a-boo with the woolly edges of her hat. She's persuasive and incisive and obscurely exotic. Experience confirms that she will use all of these talents to get her way, and likely be thanked for it too.

I adjust my zoom. Out across the dry moat stretching below this ancient fortress, they've put down, of all things, a skating rink. Twirling colors tempt my camera; seeking atmosphere, I shoot them in long-exposure black and white instead. But I find myself looking to Silke again before too long has passed. That's always the way of it. I've been so bloody attracted to her since the start. Even now, our relationship is defined by the need to be touching her skin, to possess with hands, mouth and cunt, to surrender when she needs to mark me back. Is it really any wonder that my fantasies lean toward the opportunity to touch her *more?*

She's busy chatting up the Ravenmaster—and what would that be like to fill in as occupation on a customs form?—but she turns to look at me over one shoulder like she's felt my stare warming her back. Her pleasure lights up the wintery gloom. I blossom to it, as does the gruff fellow she's charming. When she ambles back, there's the gleam of victory in her eyes and a swing in her hips that I immediately mistrust.

My breasts tighten, ache, as I lower the camera. "Right," I say. There's a throatiness to my voice we can both hear. "Hot sex and public disgrace it is."

Nothing goes to plan, of course. Silke's lilting accent and our impeccable tourist board credentials have won us the right to take as many pictures of the Bloody Tower as we would like. Only, they caught me gawking at the ravens, and as a special privilege, they'll let us borrow one for the shoot.

Marvelous. I will be a bad twist on a Lewis Carroll riddle, caught between a raven and a writing desk.

I am in trouble.

I am *very* turned on.

"Don't be nervous," she whispers as we tread well-worn cobbles in the wake of our guard.

"I'm not," I assure her, and it's true. "Just wound up."

And that's true too. Her hand, resting not-so-discreetly along the top of my bum as we walk, gives me a gentle squeeze.

He's chatty, our Beefeater, and gives us stories for Silke to take home and spin to gold. I learn that the Bloody Tower was prison not just to a famous explorer but to a whole host of colorful characters. I learn that it's bloody because it's thought to be *the* tower, the one where the boy princes were done for. I learn that not even flashbacks to grammar school history or the high likelihood of CCTV are enough to kill my undeniable and inadvisable arousal.

"The Tower may be haunted," he warns us in sepulchral tones. His comedic partner, the raven, Branwen, supplies a menacing croak from her perch on his leather armguard. He's already given us the straight-to-porn reprieve, told us that he'll be leaving us for a twenty-minute stretch while he beds down his remaining birds in their aviary outside. Silke's answering smile has put the old geezer in a good mood.

I pat my satchel of equipment. "If any vengeful spirits want to pose for the website, I'm happy to oblige."

We all laugh. I stare at Traitors' Gate as we pass, then fix my gaze ahead at the gray stones squatting before the exit to the river. The Bloody Tower. On the lower floor, it's furnished as though Sir Walter's just stepped outside for his daily constitutional and will be back to his prison diaries at any moment. Starkly white plastered stone shapes the space, leaded diamonds in the windows add charm, a tall candelabrum provides a home for Branwen to perch.

I gloss over the details once I'm satisfied there's no video, ignore the small talk of our guide as he leaves us. All my attention is fixed upon the desk I'll be bending my girlfriend across as soon as possible.

The ornate wood is high and hard. Reassuringly sturdy. There's a writing block that takes up half the desktop. It's piled with dusty books and a feather quill that gives me instant ideas, though I don't dare touch any of it. There won't be much room for her to maneuver on the small space, but it's better that way—she's a squirmer.

I pull my camera out of my satchel and flick it on since we'll need some photos for cover. While I prowl about the room,

Silke perches on the edge of the desk, swinging her legs in slow circles. The heavy heels of her boots scrape against the reddish stones of the floor. My nipples stand to attention like the guards outside.

"You're stalling," she says. "Aren't you interested in having your fantasy fulfilled?" She spreads her legs, hooking her hands underneath her knees. I make the mistake of looking. Her calves are begging for my touch while her flexibility is inspiring.

Despite my distraction, the atmosphere of this place is intense. I fancy I feel history's slow creep across my skin as I watch the raven resettle. She is positioned perfectly, light- and shadow-cooperative. Focusing each shot makes me realize just how large this bird is, how razor-sharp her claws and beak, how blue-black her feathers. Pixels do nothing to tame Branwen's power, but the susurration of Silke's coat sliding off her shoulders to the floor puts me exactly where my girlfriend wants me.

Once she has my complete attention, she drops her legs back down to the floor and pouts. "If you don't want to fuck me, just say so."

I abandon raven and reason to turn my camera on my own wild creature instead. Her heart is in her eyes, there is sex in her smile. As with the bird, watching Silke through layers of machinery and glass doesn't distance her; it brings her sharply into relief, creates an intimacy, a safe space for just the two of us. She likes the attention. I can see it in the dilation of her pupils, the way she plucks at the heavy edges of my coat. I snap in extreme close-up and capture it all.

"Oh, I'll fuck you," I assure her because there's no doubt of that now. "I'd just prefer not to spend the night in a dungeon afterward. You'd only go and hog the manacles."

She's smiling again as she says, a bit breathless, "Don't be silly. An execution might upset the school groups."

The corduroy of her skirt is inching up shapely thighs colored with thick cotton. All it will take is the nudge of my body to tip her back fully onto the polished wood. My coat swings open, swaying toward her. I don't remember unbuttoning it, and I only just remember to set my camera safely aside before I lick her mouth to share my need and taste hers.

Her arms wrap around my neck, pulling me in for a chilly kiss that warms with every stroke of tongue. She catches my bottom lip between her teeth. Worries it gently.

We hear the raven's cry of warning before the footsteps. Silke's off the desk in the nick of time as the door swings open again.

"I forgot to warn you that she's a biter," our Warder says.

I nearly give the game away with my nervous giggle. I cover by pointing to where the raven still perches. "She's being very good," I say. "An excellent subject."

He nods, blithely unsuspicious in the way of clueless blokes around women fucking, and ducks out again. He leaves the door ajar, but there's no time to close it, just as there's no time for my pulse to slow.

Silke's tugging at my scarf, pulling me back to her. She turns and bends over the desk with a showy sluttiness, from the breasts she's thrusting forward to the shimmy of her hips. I stare at her bottom.

"I do like this desk," she sighs, her voice going soft and thoughtful as she stretches across it. "All broad and...chiseled."

"And now you want to be fucked on it."

"I want *you* to fuck me on it," she corrects.

My skin prickles. "Filthy girl."

"I'm sure the desk has seen worse." She arches a little, her bum lifting as she goes up on her toes. "Raleigh was imprisoned here for *years*."

Opposite us, above the fireplace, is an oil portrait of the Bloody Tower's former occupant. I feel a twinge of sympathy toward old Walter as I flex my fingers in readiness. No doubt the ladies drove him mad too.

I shove her skirt up to her waist, the heat rising off her body tempting me to crowd closer. Her purple stockings have eyelets through which I can see little scallops of white skin. When I touch, she shivers obligingly, and I begin to work the elastic down over her thighs.

My first slap catches her flush across both cheeks, startling a cry from her that is mostly triumph, which won't do at all. I'm gentle because her skin won't be warm yet, and because we don't want to be too noisy, but soon she's turning rosy down below and breathless up above. I snare my naughty Silke around the middle, splaying my free hand across her belly. All I've got is a handful of warm winter jumper until she guides my fingers up to cup her tit.

When I slap her again, this time I let myself linger on her ass, rubbing circles over the marks I've made. The raven skitters on her perch but I don't spare her a thought because Silke's moving underneath my hands, canting herself into the edge of the table as she seeks pressure for her pubis. Letting her rock, I drape down over the invisible line of her spine, covering her with my body.

Going on tiptoe makes it easier for me to fit my hips to her ass and move with her, and I *need* it, because I've been wet for what seems like hours now. The graphic friction between cloth and cunt isn't quite enough; it drives me to seek *more* pressure. There's none to be found on the lush curves of her body, so I hitch her further across the desk, angling my hips against her ass and thigh until I find just the right spot to gratify.

Her body is beginning to shake with the effort of holding the position. I lean to stroke her throat, everything I can reach; she ducks down her chin to take my fingertips in her mouth. Warm tongue, feather-soft. I can't hold back my little groan of appreciation. She opens wider for me, her neck craning at an awkward angle made more difficult by the way I'm now pumping my fingers into her mouth.

Get them nice and wet, I don't need to say; she's a naughty girl, but she's good when she wants to be. I feel her spit coat my fingers, and that's enough—as hot as her mouth is, she'll be even better inside.

I know that I should be worrying that the Warder will return, that the raven's sounding increasingly unhappy at our backs, that this probably *is* treason. But her ass tilts up to me, and I can slide my fingers all the way along her crease from the beautiful clutch of her hole down through her honey to her stiff little clit, and honestly, I don't care. All I want to know about are those breathy noises she makes when I forget to tease her open because I'm so desperate to just plunge straight in.

Oh, *oh,* those noises. Sounds of pleasure that are so sweet against my panting breaths and the scrape of the raven's claws on iron. Silke's utterly pliant underneath me, all her curves flattened against the unforgiving table, but neither of us notices. The important thing is how her folds part against one-two-three of my fingers, how her juice burns effervescent around them, how delicious she is when I pull them out for a quick taste.

While I'm knuckle-deep in her body, her vibrancy singing through into mine, it's hard to imagine this place as a prison. Silke's the storyteller, though. She takes hold of the idea for me, like she took charge of my fantasy; gilds it into a filthy tale of serving wenches coaxed across this very desk. Cock and cunt, flung-up skirts, gasping need and traded favors—it coils with the danger to bring us to fever pitch.

From across the room, Bronwen beats her wings in agitation

across the air. But Silke's groaning now, with every thrust of my fingers. My other hand has found its way underneath her jumper, to where perspiration pools at the base of her spine. I dig my thumb into damp skin just to hear her hiss. When she does, I give her what she wants, that curl and press of blunt nails against the rough patch inside her. Her keen rings out like the raven's caw, loud to my ears, loud enough that I quiet her into silent sobs as I do it again.

The raven takes flight, battering against the leaded glass with her wings. I crane around to see, trying to keep my rhythm while I investigate the problem.

"Oops." Laughter trembles across Silke's fucked-out vowels. Then, *"Don't stop."*

"Shhh," I beg, and keep my hand moving, unable to stop touching her.

There's a legend about the ravens of the Tower of London, a portent of disaster. Should they ever leave the confines of this place, the White Tower will fall and the empire will crumble.

"Don't worry," she tells me, urging me faster with open, gasping mouth. "Can't go far. Wings...clipped."

I push in hard. With a final twist of my fingers she's coming around me with yipping cries and velvet ripples. Her legs twitch and judder, and I hold still in her, deep as I can, letting her take away all my worries and make them good.

If there *are* restless ghosts here, I hope we've given them a good show.

Silke's body is limp now, all the tension drained out of her. Her cheek slides along the surface of the desk as she lets her head hang over the edge.

We pant together for a long moment until she says, "Becky... there's gum down here."

She sounds outraged. It's hilarious, as there's a trace of her cum too on the dark wood. I lick my thumb and smudge it away. "Young vandals."

Skating my fingers along the outer folds of her cunt, I find that while she was wet when I was inside her, she's now sopping. I dip into her again, tempted for another go despite the insanity of the idea.

Then she rolls over, propping herself up on her elbow and smiling up at me muzzily. She looks *well*-fucked.

"Come here," she slurs as she hauls herself up with my scarf. I should back away, should get myself together, but right now Silke is using her booted ankles to squeeze my hips and pull me nearer. I crowd into the space between her splayed legs, letting her rub wet denim over my cunt until the friction catches fire and I come with a sharp cry and sparks against my eyelids.

Dizzy with her, it's all I can do to fumble along as her skirt pulls down and stockings go up. I'm shakily cleaning my sticky fingers on the ends of my scarf and closing my coat when I hear Silke curse. Spinning around, I expect the worst, but there's no angry Warder waiting in the doorway. There's nothing in the room but us.

"Where the *fuck* is the bird?" she demands, hands on hips.

Clipped wings, maybe, but I picture the bloody great thing hopping down the hallway, frightened off by our sex noises. I start laughing, can't stop.

It draws her back to me as she begins to laugh too. "Well, it can't have gone far. The Tower's still standing, the kingdom seems intact."

I shake my head, still breathless. "I knew you'd be trouble when I fell for you. But I never thought the British Empire would fall for you too."

Silke nibbles at my earlobe with sharp teeth. Her kiss is actually cooler than my flaming skin. "Don't worry, Becks, next time we'll just steal the Crown Jewels instead."

I grin at her. Her hat's been knocked off-kilter and the high ridges of her cheekbones are smudged with pink. I think, *Everything will be fine, as long as we've got this love.*

And I know that when we leave this fortress, we'll see the HMS *Belfast* glowing in the early evening, we'll get mesmerized by Tower Bridge like we always do. She'll tug me away from fiddling with my night settings. We'll cross down from the Hill and wander fruitlessly for an open pub until we give up and jump the Tube at Bank.

She'll jump *me* as soon as we're home. I'll try to tease her properly this time, make her wait in squirming suspense until morning, but we both know I won't be able to resist. I'll crawl down between her thighs to lick her out and she'll return the favor. We'll tangle together until I kick her over to her side of the bed. Another night we'll share another fantasy and I can only hope for my aching back that she's never had a kink for the Stone of Scone.

When we do walk out, Silke tucks her mittened hand into my pocket as we turn instinctively toward the river. Between my legs is the contrast of the cold night on my still-hot flesh. I like knowing that she'll be feeling it too.

Sod the ravens in the Tower. In the rattle and hum of this eternal city, together *we* are legend.

"So. Raleigh," I say, knotting my scarf against the wind. "Cheeky bugger by the looks of it. Laying down his cloak for saucy Liz Tudor to step on? Wonder what else he laid."

My lady grins and reaches underneath my coat to pinch my bum. "That's the spirit."

THE WAY TO A WOMAN'S HEART

Catherine Paulssen

As Matilda chopped the basil and parsley, excitement rushed to her stomach, little butterflies that ignored the chaos around her, looking forward only to sharing the night alone with Olivia. She stirred the blubbering apricot pulp that simmered in a pot next to her before continuing to hack the herbs, and her mind wandered back to the time the fluttering had started, so many years ago. They had been cramming art history for their midterm exam—no time, money or inclination to prepare something fancy—and when the rumbling in their bellies reminded them that they couldn't be wise on empty stomachs, she had made them some pasta.

The Price Chopper spaghetti, ready in less than ten minutes; a jar of Newman's Own organic tomato basil sauce her mother had left her—"So you'll at least eat something wholesome once in a while"—heated in the microwave; a chunk of Parmesan she had borrowed from her roommate, now unusable and covered in mold. The meal she had presented Olivia that day could hardly be called awe-inspiring.

For some quiet minutes, while nothing was heard but the clanging of forks against pottery bowls, she had taken her mind off Renaissance construction designs and instead studied Olivia, who had been kind enough to pretend that the slightly sticky pasta and ready-made sauce was the best food she had ever had. Her shiny dark strands had fallen onto an exquisite face, oval and dominated by a pointed chin that moved from side to side when she concentrated hard and ground her teeth. Her slender hands had moved quickly while coiling the spaghetti on her fork. She had looked up, and the probing stare of her dark eyes had struck Matilda deep inside. For longer and longer moments, she had been unable to look away—or to ignore that unfamiliar humming deep in her belly whenever their eyes met. The expression with which Olivia contemplated her had been impossible to read until her face had eased up into a boyish grin and the sobriety in her eyes had been replaced by an impish sparkle.

"Let me," she had said, reaching out and wiping away a drop of pasta sauce that had spilled on Matilda's chin, mocking her gently for her inability to eat like a grown-up.

Matilda hadn't moved as Olivia's fingers touched her skin, and for a fleeting moment, her friend was no longer the kind, funny fellow student from Professor McNeill's class. An instant later, Olivia's eyes had become unreadable again, but Matilda knew she had sensed the sensual tension too. That night, at the door of her apartment, they had said good-bye with a kiss.

Now she reached for a little bowl of grated pine nuts to mix with the herbs.

They'd been together for more than ten years, and though money was no longer something to worry about, time had again become a precious commodity. So tonight, she would once again evoke that newly-wed feeling that had gotten a little lost amidst the children's birthday parties, family gatherings, 1040 forms and overtime hours—that spark she had felt when Olivia first looked at her with that certain expression in her eyes. Matilda couldn't help the smile that curled her lips whenever she pictured the moment Olivia would return from her trip to the architects' convention and discover the luscious dinner for two that had been prepared for her, all perfect with lilies, Nina Simone and special-occasion china.

Over the years, Matilda's cooking abilities had improved, as long as the recipe wasn't too demanding. But even being a wife and mother of two with a part-time job at the Smithsonian had done nothing for her organizing skills. She figured that a selection of antipasti followed by a few simple Italian dishes would smooth over the fact that she'd never become a talent in the kitchen.

So far, she had a plate of coarse farmer salami imported from Tuscany, neatly arranged with thick slices of fresh figs, and an apricot sauce to go with the dessert.

And about four hours to go.

She sprinkled olive oil over the herbs. In those four hours, she needed to get the four-course dinner ready, set the table, decorate the bedroom and transform herself from a messy woman with a kitchen smell in her hair into a seductive beauty who would evoke memories of younger days.

Cleaning up thc kitchen was so unrealistic it wasn't even an option. She could take care of it tomorrow. And what did a messy kitchen matter anyway, as long as the bedroom was glowing in candles and fairy lights?

The phone rang, and Matilda cursed under her breath. "Hey, Mom!"

"Darling! The kids just wanted to say hello. Here you go." She heard her mother pass the phone to her son.

"Hi, Mommy."

"Hey, Bennybear!"

"Mom! I'm almost seven!"

"Okay, okay, I'm sorry, big boy. Are you having a good time?"

"Grandpa took us on a boat tour! And we saw a real Indian village."

While listening to her oldest recount the day with his grandparents, Matilda cast a glance at a pot that held six pear halves simmering in a stock of Chardonnay and spices. "That sounds fantastic!" she said, putting as much enthusiasm into her voice as possible while keeping the phone tucked between her chin and her shoulder and chopping up some anchovy fillets to blend with the herbs and pine paste.

"And guess what?" her son continued excitedly. "They have big trees. So big you can't see them end, and Grandpa says they're a thousand years old!"

"So you're having fun?" Matilda asked, distracted by a spluttering sound from another pot.

"Uh-huh. What are you going to do tonight? Will Mama be back soon?"

She turned down the burner and for a moment, indulged in the delicious smell of cream, cinnamon, lemon zest and sugar, the base for what was supposed to become panna cotta. "Yes, in a few hours. I'm making dinner for us."

"What are you having?"

Matilda sighed. "Um...pasta." If she ever got to it.

"Grandma's making us potato wedges."

That's what she should have gone for. "That's very nice, Ben. Put Lilly on the phone, okay? And have fun."

"You too!" he said happily. After some rustling at the other end of the line, her daughter's sanguine voice piped through the speaker. Her first words were lost on Matilda, who tried hard to suppress a little shriek as a squirt of hot apricot sauce burnt her finger.

"Are you lonely without us, Mommy?"

She smiled. "No, angel. I'm good. And Mama will be home soon." The butterflies fluttered excitedly as she said the words. "But I miss you."

"Grandma wants to talk to you," Lilly said.

"All right, sweetie. Have a fun weekend. And listen to Grandma and Grandpa. I love you."

"Love you too. Bye!" There was a moment's silence as Lilly handed the phone off.

"So Olivia will come back tonight?" her mother inquired.

"Uh-huh. Listen—"

"If you need some more time to yourself, we can keep the children for a few more days. They've been really good."

"No, that's fine. Actually, I'm just—"

"But you complained that you never get to do anything just the two of you!"

A pungent smell alarmed her. "Mom, I'm making dinner for us and—"

"A dinner?" Even through the phone, Matilda could see her mother's sneer. "What—cooked solely by you?"

"Yes, solely by me!" she replied defensively. "And Liv likes what I—Mom, I gotta go. Say hi to Dad."

She tossed the phone away and rushed to the oven. The pears were ruined. Sighing, she threw the burnt reminders into the trash. *One thing always has to go wrong,* she told herself. She shrugged it off, turned the music up and got out another chopping board. As she began to cut the tomatoes, she kept careful watch over the boiling cream; she couldn't lose that as well.

Her efforts paid off, and when she eventually set aside the small panna cotta–filled ramekins to cool, Matilda smiled proudly, confident the cooked cream would harden in time. Dessert and starters: check.

Next up was the pasta sauce. She was lilting along to Billie Holiday and pulling a package of mascarpone out of the fridge when a soft voice at the door made her squeal. She spun around with wide eyes. "Oh no! What are you doing here?"

Olivia leaned against the door frame, grinning widely. "I'm happy to be back too."

Matilda rolled her eyes. "Ha ha. Look around."

"Figs, baguette, some dessert sauce...and I smell cinnamon..." Olivia crossed her arms and took the kitchen in with one glance. "Are you expecting a secret lover?"

Matilda made a resigned face and shrugged. "You got me. I'm sorry you had to find out this way. She's this amazing, sexy woman, and she is supposed to come back from a convention in *three hours*."

Olivia laughed. "Come here," she whispered, and Matilda fell into her open arms.

"I missed you," she mumbled, her lips close to Olivia's. She could taste the airplane-grade tomato juice on her mouth, and the butterflies burst into applause when they kissed.

Olivia made a purring sound that Matilda took as reciprocation.

"Where are the kids? Still at Yosemite?" Olivia asked when their kiss ended.

"Uh-huh. They say hi." Matilda wrapped her arms around her wife. "Are you hungry?"

"Seeing all this? How could I not be!"

Matilda broke away from their embrace. "I'm only done with the appetizers."

"Why don't you get dressed, and I'll get us a table at Linton's?"

"No! I wanted us to..." Matilda brushed her bangs out of her face. "I wanted this to be something special. You know, just you and me." She looked at Olivia with both affection and disappointment.

Olivia threw a short look at the vegetables lying around, some cut, some peeled, most of them still waiting to be processed. She regarded the baguette that still needed to be sliced, spread and grilled, and the ingredients for the pasta sauce cluttered around the stove. Her eyes wandered to Matilda and rested on her flushed face for a while. Eventually, she reached for her hand and stroked her palm with gentle movements. "Maybe I can help?"

"No." Matilda frowned. "You just came back, and you must be exhausted. This was supposed to be a special treat. I don't want you to work on your own surprise!"

"But I messed it up by being early."

Matilda smiled a little. "You sure did! How come, anyway?"

"We finished earlier than expected, and I couldn't wait to come home, so I rebooked the flight." Olivia winked. "I thought I'd surprise you. How was I to know?"

The butterflies were dancing now, and for a moment, they made Matilda forget about being upset. "I'm sure I can have this ready in no time. You go change, or have a bath or—"

"Baby, this will take you hours!" Olivia objected. "Come on, let me help."

Matilda sighed reluctantly.

With gentle force, Olivia pulled her closer and pressed her finger on Matilda's mouth. "You will be too stressed out to enjoy any of this if you do it alone. Either you let me help, or I abduct you and carry you off to Linton's."

Matilda puckered her lips. "Seems you leave me no choice."

"You got it." Olivia kissed her tenderly. "So, tell me what to do."

"Could you cut the baguette and then spread this paste on the slices?"

"All right. I'll just get into something more comfy and be back in a minute."

Matilda watched her leave, an anthracite business suit accentuating her hourglass figure, her long legs in patent-leather pumps. A wave of her fresh, classy perfume still lingered in the air, and Matilda let her eyes wander down to her own outfit, feel-good pants and a washed-out blouse. Her hands smelled like a garlic harvester's and if she checked herself in the mirror, she would surely find traces of apricot pulp on her face. With a small sigh, she turned and started to peel an onion.

This was not how their evening was supposed to be. She hadn't set the table, the dinner would take at least another hour, and the bedroom looked far from romantic.

Olivia returned and started to prepare the crostini. "On the baking tray?" she asked, half-turned toward Matilda.

"Uh-huh," Matilda mumbled and wiped her eyes.

Olivia looked up. "Please tell me you're crying because of the onions."

Matilda nodded, sniffing. For some moments, she furiously hacked the onion into small shreds. The butterflies had stopped their dance.

"This is not how it was supposed to be." It finally burst out of her. "I wanted to look irresistible, I wanted to spoil you, I wanted all this to be ready!" She made a gesture comprising the kitchen. "It's been so long since we had a weekend to ourselves, and I wanted tonight to be perfect for you!"

Olivia didn't reply, but threw her a peculiar look from beneath her dark lashes. She placed the last piece of bread on the tin, walked over to her and clasped her hands around her waist. "Put that away for a moment," she said, taking the chopping knife and a half-cut onion out of Matilda's hands and lifting her up onto the kitchen counter. "You know the moment I knew I wanted to marry you?"

Matilda snuffled and shook her head.

Olivia pushed the chopping board away and spread Matilda's legs a bit so she could be closer to her. "It was on the second anniversary of our first kiss. Remember that night?"

Matilda wiped her cheek. "I planned to make dinner for us."

"You burnt the fish, and the rice was still raw." Olivia's eyes shimmered softly, and her voice had a tenderness to it that made her recollection of the ruined dinner sound like a declaration of love. A few butterflies fluttered their wings again.

"In the end, we had pizza from Sammy's," Matilda said and laughed. She wrapped her arms around Olivia's neck. "So how was that the day you knew you were going to marry me?"

Olivia looked down. "When you were running out of fish to turn into sad little pieces of coal and finally let me order takeout, you had this same disappointed look on your face...like a little girl who just found out the truth about Santa." She shrugged her shoulders. "I just knew." She placed her lips on Matilda's and spoke the last words directly into Matilda's mouth. "There was no one I ever wanted to kiss but you. For my whole life."

Matilda rested her head on Olivia's shoulder. "See, now you're so sweet and I missed you so much and I wanted to have the perfect night planned for us and..." She fought the tears that filled her eyes. "Instead it's a mess. And not just the food—me too."

"There's no denying it," Olivia said matter-of-factly.

The butterflies stopped and hung their wings. She hadn't exactly been fishing for compliments; after all, she *was* a mess. But a bit of sugarcoating would have helped.

Olivia moved her hand beneath Matilda's chin and raised her head. "And yet…I can't stop marveling at how hot you are." The fingers of her other hand crawled underneath Matilda's shirt and lingered there. "And you have no idea how much I want you. Right now."

Swarms of butterflies bumping into each other as they buzzed around excitedly. "You…in *this*?" Matilda tugged at her stained blouse.

Olivia nudged Matilda's upper lip with hers. "And the pants you've insisted on keeping for ages now." She let her hand wander down Matilda's jeans, making the hairs on the small of her back rise. "And you know what?" she mumbled, half kissing her.

"Mmph?"

Olivia took her time, teased Matilda's tongue with hers and nibbled a little on her bottom lip before sealing her mouth with a kiss.

"What?" Matilda wrapped her legs around Olivia's thighs.

Olivia moved her mouth toward Matilda's ears and placed little kisses on her neck. "I want to taste you," she breathed, and her damp sigh sent the butterflies over the edge for good. "You…and this…" she said, reaching for the bowl of apricot sauce. She picked up a piece of bread, dunked it in the sauce, then dipped it in mascarpone.

Matilda bit her lips. "That looks delicious."

"Taste it," Olivia whispered and watched Matilda take a bite. She ran her finger across a drop of fruit juice that was dripping down Matilda's chin and licked at her lips. "Amazing," she mumbled as her fingers unbuttoned Matilda's blouse.

Matilda dipped her finger in the creamy white mixture, then coated it with apricot sauce. She watched Olivia lick the sweet paste off her finger before melting into another long kiss. Olivia pushed her back onto the countertop and stripped off her blouse. Impatiently, Olivia fumbled with the bra and gave a satisfied sigh when she finally removed that as well. With a sparkle in her eyes that made the butterflies delirious with anticipation, she held the bowl of sauce over Matilda's bare chest and half-naked body. "It's the only thing we really need," she whispered. The next moment, thick drops of fruit sauce were running down Matilda's nipples.

Matilda sighed and pushed back her head. She closed her eyes and moaned softly when Olivia's tongue started to lick off the juice. Olivia's fingers crawled up her body, searching for her mouth. They were sticky and tasted of cream and apricots. Matilda kissed them, then ran her lips down Olivia's palm and wrist. But when she made a move to sit up, she was forced down by a flat hand. A cool sensation followed the wild strokes of Olivia's tongue as she adorned the tip of Matilda's breasts with mascarpone. Soft quivers made the paste wobble on her hardened nipples.

"Watch," Olivia said, and Matilda propped herself up to watch her draw a big heart on her belly. The curtain of Olivia's black hair was blocking Matilda from seeing her lap off the line of apricot sauce, and she brushed back the strands, sticky with fruit juice.

Olivia kissed Matilda's belly button and made a noise of pleasure. "Baby, you are so lickable." Her fingers opened the zipper of Matilda's pants. "In fact..." She pulled the pants away. Her finger moved over Matilda's panties and teasingly, she increased the pressure the farther down she went. She didn't waste much time before allowing the panties to follow the rest of Matilda's clothes onto the floor.

"Thank you for loving me the way you do," Olivia whispered, and now Matilda did sit up. She pressed a fierce and loving kiss on Olivia's mouth that transformed into a stifled moan as Olivia's finger began to rub her. The bottle of olive oil toppled over with a clunk as Olivia made her lie back again. Matilda could feel the velveteen liquid somewhere underneath her shoulders, but soon, all other feelings were ousted by the humming of a jubilant ballet of butterflies, which turned more and more into an uncoordinated bop with every caress of Olivia's tongue.

When the tension grew too much to bear, she began to scream. The sound soon morphed into a long moan as Olivia's lips caused her to climb that last edge and fall down on the other side.

She remained lying there, her eyes closed, the olive oil slippery underneath her back now, and despite her numbness, she could feel Olivia's breath warm and damp against her thigh. She shivered a bit as Olivia got up and rested her head on her belly. Matilda wondered if her wife could feel the butterflies bowing graciously, taking a deep breath and preparing for the next dance.

Languidly, she twirled one of Olivia's strands around her finger. "That was so not what I had in mind when I pictured the evening."

Olivia laughed. "Disappointed?"

Matilda shook her head. "Not at all."

Olivia snuggled her head into the curve of her belly and drew circles on her skin. She pressed a kiss on Matilda's belly, then wrapped her sticky, sweaty, languid body into her arms. "Neither am I."

RIPPLES IN STILL WATER

Stella Harris

Melanie came through the door, dropped her gym bag and squatted down to receive enthusiastic kisses from Bandit, her Boston terrier. Once his need for affection was sated she moved further into the house, looking for her wife Ruby. At this time of night she expected to find her in bed, propped up on pillows and reading a book. But as she rounded the turn into the hallway, Melanie was met by humid air and the smell of lavender—Ruby was running a bath.

The wave of fondness she felt at the thought of her wife lounging in bubbles, pampering herself, was quickly overcome by a flutter of panic in her gut. She didn't like the idea of Ruby getting in and out of the bath on her own, especially when she was in the house by herself.

"Ruby?" she called out, as much to announce herself as to actually find Ruby. The last thing she needed was to startle her while she was in a precarious position. She'd never forgive herself if Ruby was hurt because of her.

"In here." Ruby's voice came from the bathroom.

Melanie, in the room just a few steps later, was relieved to find Ruby sitting on the closed toilet, still bundled in the heavy terry-cloth robe she'd given her last winter.

"Hey," Ruby said, smiling up at her.

"Hey yourself." Melanie bent over to give Ruby a lingering kiss before preparing to let loose about how dangerous it was for Ruby to be taking a bath alone, but Ruby cut her off.

"Don't lose your head, I knew you'd be home tonight and I was waiting for you to get here." Ruby spoke with her usual resigned annoyance. Melanie had been fussing since the day they found out Ruby was pregnant, and while she claimed to hate Melanie's mother-hen routine, Melanie secretly suspected she enjoyed the attention.

At Ruby's admission, Melanie relaxed. She squatted and rested her hands on Ruby's thighs. "How are you feeling?"

"I'm feeling perfectly fine—same answer I texted you a few hours ago." Ruby's smile took the bite out of her words. Melanie squeezed her thighs, giving her a playful leer and parting her bathrobe. She got further than she'd expected before Ruby batted her hands away. "Now that you're here, how about you make yourself useful and help me into the tub?"

Melanie offered Ruby her hands, and Ruby stood a little awkwardly but didn't complain about her center of gravity being off. A familiar refrain, but Melanie didn't mind. She wouldn't be nearly as gracious as Ruby if she were the one whose body was going through these changes.

Ruby untied her belt and let the robe fall to the floor around her feet. Melanie wanted to tell her how beautiful she was, but knew Ruby was self-conscious about her new, curvier form and didn't always respond well to compliments. Instead she made herself as unobtrusive as possible, ready to offer whatever support Ruby needed as she stepped carefully into the tub, first one foot and then the other.

Melanie waited until Ruby was settled comfortably, knelt beside the tub, and grabbed the washcloth and soap. She dunked the cloth into the tub and lathered it up while Ruby leaned back and closed her eyes. Ruby liked to act tough, but Melanie knew she didn't enjoy the weekends she spent alone while Melanie was out of town working. It had been bad enough being apart before, but now that Ruby was pregnant it was even worse. Melanie hated being away just as much, but they needed the money, especially now, with a baby on the way.

Once the washcloth was soapy enough, Melanie massaged Ruby's shoulders and neck. A look of bliss crossed Ruby's face and she sank a few inches deeper into the tub. With her short frame she could actually stretch out in the tub and be fully covered by the water, the only thing that Melanie envied about Ruby's height.

"So how was work?" Ruby asked after basking in the massage. The degree of pleasure Ruby took in hearing about Melanie's—or more accurately, Whiskey's—customers was difficult to fathom. She could still remember how terrified she'd been about telling Ruby what she did when they first met. The last thing she expected was that the perky tea-shop barista she'd had her eye on for weeks not only wouldn't mind that she was a stripper, but that she'd be fascinated by it. To this day Ruby had never actually gone to a club to watch her work, but she loved hearing all the details.

"Work was work, nothing out of the ordinary," Melanie said, urging Ruby to lean forward so she could scrub her back. She had stories to tell, of course, but she liked to tease and make Ruby work for it. It had gotten to the point that she would compose her stories in advance while she was working—thinking of the best way to describe a particular customer or a new dancer. It made work more interesting, especially when things were slow.

"You're holding out on me," Ruby grumbled.

Melanie smiled and got up on her knees, leaning forward so she could reach all of Ruby's back. "Well, there was one guy who kept talking about pickles...dills, gherkins, bread-and-butter...he asked each girl what her favorite kind of pickle was, and each time he was disappointed with the answer."

"What did you say?"

"I told him I didn't like pickles."

Ruby flicked water at her. "That's not true, you love pickles! You have more pickle cravings than I do, and I'm the pregnant one!"

"True, but that's me. Whiskey doesn't like pickles." Ruby made her "thinking face" at this, her eyebrows pulling together. Melanie thought this was painfully cute, but had learned the hard way not to comment on it.

"Okay, that's fair," Ruby conceded. "How else is Whiskey different from you?"

"Well, for one thing she doesn't have a hot wife waiting for her at home."

Ruby stuck her tongue out at that, but didn't argue with the compliment. The warm water seemed to be relaxing some of the feistiness out of her.

"Actually, I did break my rule. I told one of my customers about you."

Ruby perked up at this. "Really?"

"Yeah, this girl came in with her husband and she was really sweet. Bought a lot of dances and we started chatting. I'm not sure what it was about her, but I just started talking, telling her about my life."

"Did you tell her your real name?"

"No, I didn't go that far. There are some rules I don't break," Melanie assured her.

"So tell me about this girl. Was she as sexy as me?"

"No one's as sexy as you." That earned Melanie more water flicked in her direction, but Ruby didn't manage to quash her smile before Melanie had seen it.

"So what did she look like?" Ruby leaned forward as she asked, presenting her back for more attention. Melanie lathered up the cloth again and went to work as she spoke.

"She was tall, taller than me, even with my heels. Shoulder-length red hair in a bob. Slender, but with curves in the right places." Melanie took her chances and punctuated the word *curves* by dipping her hands under the water and grasping Ruby's hips—always deliciously curvy and even rounder than usual over the last few months. Ruby didn't protest, so Melanie kept her arms under the water, squeezing Ruby's hips and digging her thumbs into Ruby's lower back.

"So? That's all it took to make you spill your story? Red hair and some curves?" Ruby teased.

"Not just that. She had a great laugh and seemed interested in what I had to say. Even when I was completely nude, she was still looking me in the eye—that's not something I encounter much, even with the female customers."

"You don't get girls much. Was it fun dancing for her?"

"Sort of, certainly more fun than a creepy old guy with wandering hands. But it hit a little too close to home. I don't want to enjoy myself at work, it spoils my concentration."

"So you enjoyed yourself, huh? Did she turn you on?" Ruby's voice dropping low. Melanie knew this wasn't a test. Neither of them was the jealous type.

"A little bit, yeah. She had great breasts..." Melanie let her story trail off as her hands wandered, cupping Ruby's swollen breasts as she spoke. She loved feeling the weight of them, loved how they'd become more sensitive. Ruby complained about it sometimes, on days when even wearing a bra made her uncomfortable, but she didn't complain about it in bed, when Melanie sucked on her nipples until she writhed and moaned.

Melanie felt herself grow wet at the thought. It had only been four days since she'd been with Ruby, but that was long enough for her to ache with missing her. She let her thumbs brush over Ruby's nipples until they hardened under her touch. The combination of water and arousal made her nipples crinkle as they swelled into hard nubs.

Ruby caught her bottom lip between her teeth, another habit that Melanie adored. It was a surefire sign that Melanie's advances were welcome, that Ruby was in the mood to enjoy herself.

"Telling her about you wasn't the only rule I broke." Melanie sat forward on her knees to lean further over the bath. With Ruby in such a rare mood, she decided to embellish her story. "I touched her far more than I should have. She was so responsive—almost as much as you. I couldn't help myself."

"What did you do?" Ruby's eyes closed, her voice barely more than a whisper.

"Besides touch her breasts?" Melanie made another teasing sweep of her thumbs. "I bit her on the neck, like this..." Melanie brought her mouth to Ruby's neck, savoring the scent of her mixed with the lavender of the bath. She licked the moisture from Ruby's skin before pressing down with her teeth, just hard enough to reach the edge of pain and then easing off, teasing at the marks her teeth had left with her tongue. Ruby's head fell to the side, allowing her free access. She took advantage of the offer, nibbling at the length of Ruby's neck, working her way up to Ruby's ear.

Taking the lobe into her mouth, she sucked, worrying it with her teeth. Hearing Ruby's intake of breath, she worked her way up to nibble on the shell of her ear. Ruby's hands came up to meet Melanie's, her skin already getting waterlogged.

"You're pruning up. Let's get you out of here." Melanie pulled away and was met with a whimper of protest. Once Ruby was standing safely on the bath mat, Melanie wrapped the towel around her, rubbing it vigorously and eliciting a girlish giggle. Her hair was pinned loosely on top of her head, so they didn't need to worry about drying it. All the better—they could go straight to bed.

Ruby was sleepy-snuggly, one of Melanie's favorite Ruby moods. Ruby allowed Melanie to help her to the bed without a single word of protest and even lay back on the bed still naked. With her recent self-consciousness, Ruby seldom stayed naked longer than absolutely necessary, and Melanie missed looking at her.

Ruby's permanently tanned skin had a pinkish hue from soaking in the hot water, and she was soft and moist to the touch, partly from her ridiculously good genes and partly from the bath oil she'd used. Sensing that Ruby was in the mood to be touched, Melanie grabbed the bottle of lotion from the nightstand and squirted a pump into her hand. She settled on the bed and pulled one of Ruby's feet into her lap. Ruby sighed, stretching out like a kitten in the sun.

Melanie worked the foot between her hands, giving each toe her undivided attention before digging her thumbs into the arch of Ruby's foot, making her squirm. Ruby made it known when it was time for her other foot to receive the same treatment by pulling the first foot away and sliding the other into Melanie's lap. With a smile, Melanie went through the same routine with the other foot. Ruby's feet were almost perfectly smooth—she was spending less time on her feet these days and at Melanie's urging she'd accepted a bit of pampering, even submitting to a pedicure.

"You're not naked enough," Ruby complained, wiggling her feet and then shoving Melanie off the bed.

Throwing a playful glare in Ruby's direction, Melanie began to strip out of her clothes as Ruby watched from her place on the bed. Melanie didn't make a show of it. Ruby liked to tease her, and considering what she did for a living she might have been more of an exhibitionist at home, but that wasn't who she was. Putting on a show was work—when she was being herself, things like dressing and undressing were simply utilitarian.

Still, with Ruby's eyes on her she slowed her pace as she removed her bra and then her panties, sliding them down her thighs at a deliberate pace. She felt different like this, more exposed and vulnerable under Ruby's gaze than she did in front of a room full of strangers. But they didn't really see her, not the way Ruby did. And she didn't care what those strangers thought of her—it was Ruby whose opinion mattered.

She finished undressing, leaving her clothes in a pile on the floor, and crawled back into the bed, starting at the foot and working her way up. She moved carefully, trying not to jostle Ruby or put too much weight on her body. As soon as she could reach, Ruby grabbed her by the arms and pulled her into a careful embrace, tugging until she was close enough to kiss.

Aside from their quick greeting, this was their first kiss in days and Melanie savored it: the soft press of Ruby's lips, the glide of her tongue, the taste of her. Finally, she was *home*. But she wanted to do more than just kiss. Ruby was being so receptive Melanie had every intention of taking advantage. The more Ruby's belly swelled, the less often she felt sexy, and Melanie's assurances that she was as beautiful and appealing as ever fell on deaf ears.

With Ruby still breathless from their kisses, Melanie slid lower, licking and sucking at Ruby's neck again. Ruby tilted her head back, submitting to Melanie's attentions as Melanie took her time, savoring the taste of Ruby's skin, the soft texture against her lips. She reveled in the way Ruby shifted restlessly, her breath growing shallow.

Taking advantage of her distraction, Melanie slid a hand between their bodies, balancing most of her weight precariously on one arm, and found Ruby already slick and wet, her body easily accepting the press of Melanie's fingers. Ruby shifted, spreading her legs further.

Sliding lower still, Melanie worked her way down Ruby's body, kissing all the soft, tender places she found on the way. Her belly button, once tucked neatly away, now pushed outward, and Melanie placed a quick, teasing kiss there. As Melanie explored, Ruby pressed down on her shoulders, guiding her to where she wanted her to be. Ruby had a tendency to get impatient, but Melanie didn't mind, she liked a girl who knew what she wanted.

That was one of the first things that had attracted her to Ruby all those years ago. Even as a barista she'd had a take-charge attitude, and her coworkers instinctively listened to her. Ruby'd also gotten tired of waiting for Melanie to make a move and had asked her out after yet another day of flirting. Melanie loved that she never knew quite what to expect from her.

But what she liked most of all was the way Ruby took charge in the bedroom. Melanie liked knowing that she was giving her partner exactly what she wanted, and Ruby's self-assurance made it easy for Melanie to learn her body, to learn what she liked.

When she finally reached the crux of Ruby's thighs, Melanie buried her face in the dark curls she found there, where the smell of Ruby clung and lingered. Finally, *finally,* she was able to lose herself in the taste of Ruby filling her mouth.

She let all the voices in her mind fall silent and gave herself over to sensation. The way Ruby's inner walls felt contracting around her fingers, the way her body shifted and her hips arched forward. Ruby's hands tangled up in her hair, pulling and directing her just exactly how she wanted.

Melanie let herself be used. She slid her free hand between her own legs and rode her fingers to the pace of Ruby's thrusting hips. Her attention was torn between Ruby's pleasure and her own. Ruby grabbed at her again, tugging and pulling until Melanie crawled back up Ruby's body, meeting her in a deep, desperate kiss, letting Ruby lick her own taste out of Melanie's mouth.

Ruby's hair had escaped from its fastenings and spilled across the pillow as she'd turned her head side to side. She looked like something out of a romantic painting, the spill of her hair a symbol of her debauched state. As much as Melanie loved to lick and suck at Ruby until she came, nothing was better than being face-to-face. She loved to watch Ruby's reactions flit across her face as she touched her, the way she'd bite her lip or squeeze her eyes closed when Melanie did something she really enjoyed.

Best of all was being face-to-face when Ruby had an orgasm. Melanie never got tired of watching as Ruby's mouth fell open, her eyes widened in surprise, her head tilted back as far as her neck would allow. She got a front-row seat for that show now, as all of the muscles in Ruby's body tensed up and a barely audible moan escaped from her bite-swollen lips.

Melanie kept stroking her until Ruby pushed her hand away

and then relaxed beside her on the bed. Her own arousal nearly forgotten, Melanie was ready to fall asleep at Ruby's side, simply grateful to be sharing a bed again.

But Ruby had other ideas. She turned on her side to face Melanie, head propped up on one bent arm, her other hand free to explore. Melanie's skin was still sensitive and Ruby's touch gave her chills, her nipples peaking at the slightest touch.

"You know, I don't think I'd have as much restraint as Whiskey," Ruby said in a contemplative voice as she stroked Melanie's body.

"Oh?" Melanie wondered where this was going.

"Faced with a gorgeous girl who had the hots for me? I bet I'd cross all sorts of lines," Ruby continued, pinching Melanie's nipple and making her gasp.

"What would you do?"

"I'd touch her," Ruby said, pinching Melanie's other nipple. "And tease her," she continued, cupping Melanie's breast and testing the weight in her hand. "And maybe, if she was wearing a skirt, I'd do this..." Ruby slid her hand between Melanie's legs.

Early in the relationship Ruby mourned Melanie's lack of pubic hair—a necessity for her job—but she'd eventually come around to the benefits of smooth-shaven skin. As her hand slid unobstructed across Melanie's moist flesh, she was very glad of it.

"I think it would be fun, see how much I could get away with before she stopped me, or before someone noticed.

"Do you think I could make a girl come in one of the private booths without anyone noticing?" Melanie's head flooded with images of Ruby scantily clad and gyrating on someone's lap. She parted her legs further as Ruby spoke, granting her easier access. Melanie's body was strung tight, but Ruby wasn't using enough pressure to bring her release. Melanie moaned, Ruby was teasing her beyond endurance. “Please,” Melanie whispered.

“Please what, baby?” Ruby teased her with feather-light strokes to her clit.

“More.” Melanie grabbed Ruby’s wrist and tried to apply more pressure where she needed it. But Ruby quickly shifted in her grip, bringing Melanie’s hand above her head, then bringing her other hand up too.

“Hold still,” Ruby instructed, and Melanie did as she was told. Seemingly satisfied that Melanie was going to obey, Ruby resumed her torment. She slid her fingers deep inside, crooking them up until Melanie gasped and arched into the touch, then pulling out again. She thrust in and out several more times before returning her attention to Melanie’s clit, making Melanie whimper.

“I suppose if I was going to try it, the girl would have to be very obedient,” Ruby continued, as though she’d never been interrupted. “She’d have to hold still and be quiet...do you think you could do that for me?” Melanie hurried to nod her assent. “Good girl.” Ruby pinched Melanie’s clit between two fingers—testing her—but Melanie didn’t cry out.

Ruby leaned close to Melanie, close enough to whisper in her ear, “I’d get very close, so close my lips brushed her ear, and tell her all the naughty things I’d do if we had more privacy, if we were somewhere that I could make her scream.”

Melanie’s body tensed, straining toward Ruby’s hand.

“I’d need to make her promise that she could come quietly. Do you think you can do that? Come without making a sound?” As Ruby spoke, she finally touched Melanie with more force, pushing her over the edge with just a few strokes.

Melanie opened her mouth in a silent scream, her back arching off the bed. Her orgasm lasted longer than any she could remember. Ruby ran her fingers through the flood of wetness between Melanie's legs, touching her until she pressed her legs together and rolled on her side to face Ruby.

Ruby was looking at her, eyes bright and smiling widely. "You don't have to be so careful with me, you know. I'll tell you what I need."

Melanie smiled too. She needn't have worried so much. Ruby was the same take-charge girl she'd always been.

WOMEN AND SONG

Rowan Elizabeth

Hand me the orange juice, would you?"

"Did you do the math on the vodka?" she asks.

"Yes," I tell her. The pitcher of Sex on the Beach is coming together nicely. "All we need is forty ice cubes."

"Seriously? Are you really going to count them?" Julia looks sideways at me and grins. An ice cube could melt in that grin. Her bright blue eyes tease me.

"Maybe." I grab my wooden spoon and swat her on the ass before I set to mixing the juicy concoction.

Spring has hit full force and we need something fruity and fun to replace our heavy red wine of the winter. I pour a mug of my favorite summer drink and offer it to the lips of my lover. "Drink."

"Why me first?"

"Because this is my witch's brew and you're my subject."

"Your lab rat?"

"Maybe."

She takes a sip.

She takes another.

It's no small task to get Julia to succumb to a tropical whim, but she walks with her mug back to her guitar sheet music.

She makes me smile.

I reach into the kitchen cabinet for a large plastic tumbler and fill it. I want to sit by the sun of the open window and draw. Having inspiration finally hit after several dry months, I'm happy to find my art coming back to me. Julia sits at the dining table with stacks of guitar magazines and sheet music. Her passion is the music that melts my bones.

I reach for a charcoal pencil and start to play with my paper. I recall a woman's face from a three-minute porn clip we'd watched that morning. Dark hair with long braids. She was the suppler of the two women. She whirled under the stronger woman's ministrations. Two minutes into the video I begged Julia to touch me as the softer woman was being touched.

"Quickly. Before breakfast."

Julia rolled me onto my back and looked at me as her right hand skimmed down my round belly. She gently pushed my legs apart and strummed her long guitar fingers, over my swelling mound, pushing her middle finger against my clit.

I hummed against Julia's neck. My eyes screwed shut against the intensity of her fingers and my hips rose. Julia worked a second finger between my lips and clipped my clit between them. I knew I would come quickly if I pressed it. Instead, I melted back into the cotton sheets to linger.

Julia eliminated my plans by sliding her fingers into my pussy and reached for my hot spot. My back arched and I ground my crotch against her hand. I spread my lower lips with my left fingers and began to stroke myself, to Julia's delight. I felt the orgasm swimming in my belly, swirling and curling to the rhythmic pressure.

We created an orgasm of color and light, streaming from my pussy.

"Baby?"

"Baby?"

I blink hard into the sun and turn to Julia. "Yes?"

"You're not drawing."

"You're not playing," I counter.

"Maybe I should."

"Maybe you should." I smile a warm smile toward my lover.

I press my pencil into the curves of the girl's braids as Julia arranges her microphone and grabs her guitar. Julia uses her thick voice and a Blind Melon song to fill the space. A melancholy song filled with pain and hope. I ask her to sing it again for me. The song fills the drawn girl's eyes with light and emotion.

I'm warm in my art, music and drink. I slip upstairs to put on a tank top in the growing heat. I pull my shirt over my head and free my breasts from my bra. I look down my body at my heavy breasts and full belly. Long legs and painted toes take me to the floor. How she loves this body to pieces amazes me. But she does, and I actually feel sexy with her.

Back downstairs, it's the intro to Sheryl Crow's "Steve McQueen." Her music pages stick together and I watch her fight with the paper.

"Fuck."

I giggle behind her and Julia flips me the bird behind her back. It makes me giggle harder.

We laugh a lot, Julia and I.

She starts the song over after a few minutes of fiddling around. Sheryl's words flow with the inspired strumming of the guitar.

I'm so inspired by her. I sit down and slide my tank over my head. Julia's back is to me as she sings and strums. I pick up my charcoal and shade the girl's jawline.

She sings a touch of Melissa and I wipe my charcoal fingers on my breasts. I blend and blot as she hums through a Band Perry song. "You Lie" dances in my head as I add bangs to my girl's forehead. My hands are covered with black dust just as Julia's are covered with calluses. The very idea of the roughness of those hands on my skin sends a shudder through me.

As I take a drink of my brew, I watch her. Her simple beauty takes my breath away each time her long blond hair sways with her body. She's so into her music that her eyes are shut tight, like when she comes. I swallow hard with the thought.

After she finishes "Me and Bobby McGee," she reaches for her mug of beach drink.

"You know, babe," Julia says, "this is some tasty stuff." She crosses the living room and leans down to kiss me.

Without thinking, I cup her face in my dusty black hand. I shut my eyes and feel her lips and tongue. The kiss that began as a simple act of affection becomes more so quickly.

"When did you take off your top?" Julia asks against my neck as she kisses her way to my ear.

"I got hot."

"I'd say."

Julia brings her mouth to my left breast and I slither my dirty hand into her freshly washed hair. Her nipping on my breast causes my pussy to react immediately. She's had that talent since the beginning.

We'd met in college. My first-semester English lit class, she sat behind me. We were so young. She'd sing the B-52s' "Love Shack" and hum songs I can still hear. We talked easily from the start and I was thrilled when she invited me to Guru Java, a little coffee-shop-live-music venue, to watch her play. She sang Sarah McLachlan with a husky voice that blended beautifully with the lyrics. Julia sang the songs of the time. Indigo Girls and Melissa Etheridge. I fell in love mid-way through "Brave and Crazy."

After, she walked me to her apartment and we drank Little Kings on her porch. She had a red Doberman named Tequila who took an instant liking to me and the fact I would throw her tennis ball over and over. I threw that ball for hours just to sit there with Julia and get drunk.

The sun rose on us asleep in the old Mexican hammock hanging on the porch. I had to pee something fierce and struggled out of the hammock and into Julia's house and found the bathroom. As I wandered back to the porch, I took a look around. She had an array of musical accouterments taking over the living room. Evidently, she played the electric and bass guitars as well as her acoustic. The air smelled heavy of incense and cheap candles. What hit me most was the light. No windows were covered with more than a gauzy film of curtain. I instantly wanted to set up my easel by the big bay window and draw.

I couldn't imagine leaving. After a quick two months, I didn't.

I'm jerked back to the moment by a pinch and tug on my nipple.

"Daydreaming while I seduce you, were you?" Julia scolds lightly.

I drop my eyes and smile through the mess of my hair. "Guilty."

"Just for that, I'm going to play another song and let you get back to your drawing."

"Rotten."

"Yep." Julia steps back with just as much charcoal dust on

her as I have on me, smeared by kisses and gentle fondling. She looks like the Coal Miner's Daughter with blond hair.

"Sing some Loretta," I ask.

Julia belts out "Alone with You."

I stretch in the sun that cascades through the windows. We still have only gauzy curtains, and our home smells of sage and white jasmine. "Alone with You" comes to a tittering halt.

"You kill me when you stretch like that." Julia gently places her worn guitar on its stand and comes to me.

I curl my legs underneath me to make room for her on the chaise. She bought me this chaise so that I could lie by the window in the sun. Its foot is covered in the remnants of charcoal, pastels and paint from my sitting on it to create. I love it. I love her.

Julia pulls the sheer drapes closed in a false sense of propriety. She lays me back on the red velvet and smiles. I stretch out my legs to allow her to crawl up my body. The chaise is too narrow for us side by side, but perfect for her above me. Her hair swings and she drags it up my belly and across my breasts.

I wrap my arms around her middle as her lips hit mine, crushing her to me. The familiarity of her body against mine, her heat and her scent make me swim in excitement. There are times we are still nineteen and crazy, but there are more times like this. Times when we are forty and comfortable. Her taste is always her, even hidden behind peach schnapps and orange juice. I am the me I've become. No longer lean and lithe but rounder and soft.

Julia pushes herself up on her arms and looks at me. She can read the look in my eyes. So she swings a leg over me and helps me up by the hand. That same callused hand holds mine as we walk down the hall to our bedroom. I sit on the edge of the bed and Julia strips off her T-shirt. She uses it to wipe some of the charcoal smudges from my breasts and then chucks the tee in the hamper.

"I want to finish what we started this morning," she whispers.

Julia gently pushes me back on the bed with a strong hand to my sternum and begins to yank at my jeans. I lift my ass off the bed and she slides them down my legs to drop them on the floor. I'm dirty and sweaty and she buries her face between my breasts. I gave up being self-conscious a long time ago. She loves my sweat and dirt. Says it's my creative juices she smells and tastes.

My head lolls back into the pillows and I absorb her.

Julia sucks my nipples one at a time. It's my left that sends the shards of excitement to my pussy. She knows that. She knows everything I love, and she begins to do them in succession. Her mouth runs over the swell of my belly, teeth gently tugging at the navel piercing I've never been able to give up. She clasps my hands in hers. We twine our fingers and she controls me.

When she nudges at my bush with her nose, I giggle. Julia looks up from between my legs with an ornery smile and makes a production of diving in. I gasp at the contact of her open mouth with my lips. It never ceases to excite me, that moment.

I wiggle and strain under her work on me. There are moments I want to come immediately and return the favor. Then there are the times, like these, that I want to feel every lap of her tongue and kiss of her lips—every darting motion and every suck, and wallow in it forever.

Julia lets go of my left hand and fixes herself more firmly between my legs. The thrust of her fingers into my wetness makes my body jerk. I know she'll find the spot that makes me squirm like a wanton woman. And she does.

In perfect precision, she works my G and sucks my clit. I arch my back and groan with the joy of it. My orgasm builds, my legs tightening along with my belly.

Julia is merciless when she feels my legs grab her. The orgasm grows and ebbs and grows stronger just before I grab her hair and cry out. It seems to last forever, and for the first time in a while, I see colors. Beautiful colors.

The first potent climax subsides for the briefest of moments before Julia clamps down to suck out the last vestiges of my orgasmic self. I shriek a sound that will probably rattle the neighbors.

As I collapse into our tossed cotton sheets, Julia looks triumphant.

"I—" I begin.

"Yes, my wonderful?"

"Colors. I saw colors this time."

"Did you hear a song?"

"No."

Julia smiles broadly and crawls up to curl up with me. "We'll have to work on that."

FULL CIRCLE

Chris Paynter

Woodstock Music and Art Fair, Bethel, New York, 1969

The mid-August air was thick with humidity, as if it were a living, breathing entity. Like if you stabbed it with a knife, the sky would bleed rain.

Jessie Roman wished it would rain, anything to cut into this heat. Even at almost two in the morning, it was oppressive. What bothered her more, though, was she was down to her last joint. She thought she'd rolled enough. But her "friends," who seemed to grow with each passing hour of the music festival, helped deplete her supply. She laughed to herself. She shouldn't be too concerned—the contact high alone was enough to send her soaring.

She ran her fingers through her short, dark, sweat-drenched hair. She was still grooving to the music, despite how miserable she felt. Creedence Clearwater Revival were not disappointing the mob of fans.

Her gaze drifted away from the stage and into the crowd. She skimmed over the writhing throng, pausing to watch a pair of topless women dance, their eyes closed and arms thrown above their heads as they bumped and grinded to the throbbing beat. Continuing her slow scan of the revelers, she suddenly stopped when she spotted a goddess—at least that's what Jessie saw in the beauty with waist-length, auburn hair.

The woman appeared to be Jessie's height of five-six or so. Her face was pale and chiseled, as if a sculptor had chipped away at the cold stone until he'd perfected the angles of this godlike countenance. Her cheekbones were sharp and defined. Her chin had a slight cleft. Jessie's finger twitched just thinking of running it down her cheek to caress that dip. Her lips were lush and full, her eyes luminous as they captured the psychedelic lighting that emanated from the stage.

The goddess's lips twitched in amusement, and Jessie looked to see what had caused that smile. It was the same bare-breasted women who had captured Jessie's attention. She grinned again at the dancers' carefree attitude. And why shouldn't they be carefree? Why the hell not dance from the sheer joy of the music and living in the moment?

She looked back at the goddess, and her breath hitched. The auburn-haired beauty was staring at her, the raw hunger in her eyes almost making Jessie fall to her knees.

Was it an invitation? Or was the high she was feeling making her think so?

As Jessie contemplated the question, the announcer brought Janis Joplin on as the next performer. Jessie watched as Joplin strolled to the microphone. She said some words to the crowd before launching into "Raise Your Hand."

But even Joplin couldn't keep Jessie from searching the crowd again for her goddess. She was still staring at Jessie.

That's it.

Without taking her eyes off the woman, Jessie said to her friend Marla, "I think I see someone I know."

Marla didn't even look at her. "Go do what you got to do, man," she shouted over the music.

Jessie shouldered her way through the sweaty horde to get to her destination. She only hoped the goddess hadn't moved. A gap in the crowd miraculously appeared...and there she stood, stunning in a purple tie-dyed dress that accentuated her full breasts, her nipples clearly visible as they pressed against the thin material.

Jessie forced her feet to keep moving until she stopped directly in front of her. Rendered speechless, she fell willingly into the pale blue depths of the woman's eyes.

Say something, you idiot. She's waiting for you to speak.

The woman held out her hand and smiled. "Come on. Let's enjoy Janis."

That simple move was all it took. Jessie let go of all her insecurities and grasped her hand.

The woman spun Jessie around to stand in front of her, her arms tight around Jessie's waist. She pressed her lips against Jessie's ear. "I'm Audrey."

"I'm Jessie." Jessie leaned back into Audrey, relishing the feel of Audrey's breasts as they pushed into her back.

No more words were spoken as Joplin ran through her set list. But as Joplin sang the opening line of "Try (Just a Little Bit Harder)," Audrey's fingers worked their way under Jessie's tank top and brushed the underside of Jessie's breasts. Jessie glanced around to see if anyone was watching. *Hell, it's Woodstock*, she thought, *and no one gives a damn.*

Audrey said into Jessie's ear, "Is this cool?"

Jessie barely nodded. Audrey immediately cupped her breasts, her thumbs tweaking Jessie's nipples. Joplin wailed while Audrey cradled one of Jessie's breasts, her other hand drifting down to the snap on Jessie's jeans. She again paused and pressed her lips against Jessie's neck. "Do you want me to stop?"

"No. God, no," Jessie croaked.

In one swift and adept move, Audrey unsnapped Jessie's jeans and worked the zipper down until she could cup Jessie through her panties. Jessie felt Audrey smile against her neck.

"You're already so wet." Audrey pushed Jessie's panties aside and delved into her slick folds. Jessie jerked when Audrey found her clit, hard and throbbing, just as Joplin cried about trying "just a little bit harder." But Audrey didn't stay there. She teased Jessie incessantly while Joplin's voice pounded into Jessie's very core.

"Listen to her," Audrey crooned. She bit Jessie's neck and then licked where her teeth had surely left their mark. "Get lost in the words."

She pinched Jessie's nipple as her fingers renewed their assault on Jessie's clit. The beginning stirrings of Jessie's orgasm moved in time with Audrey's touch.

"Feel it. Feel it down to your bones, Jessie."

Joplin screamed, "Try, oh yeah!"

Jessie's climax seemed to last an eternity. Audrey kept going as Joplin held that note. Jessie screamed right along with Joplin and exploded into another orgasm. She sagged in Audrey's arms, and Audrey's tight grip kept her from crashing to her knees.

Audrey withdrew her hand and zipped up Jessie's jeans. She gently squeezed Jessie's breast one last time before tugging her tank top back into place. Then she turned Jessie around, and without a word, claimed Jessie's mouth in a bruising kiss.

She pulled away and brushed a wet strand of hair off Jessie's forehead. "We're going to be good together."

Jessie could only smile.

Democratic National Convention, Madison Square Garden, New York, 1992

"...I end tonight where it all began for me—I still believe in a place called Hope. God bless you, and god bless America."

Bill Clinton stepped away from the podium and acknowledged the cheers from the crowd. Fleetwood Mac's "Don't Stop (Thinking About Tomorrow)" blared from the speakers. He held out his hands for his wife, Hillary, and daughter, Chelsea, who walked toward him from the side of the stage.

Audrey Cartwright viewed the scene from one of the arena's mega video screens above them. She still couldn't believe she'd gone from a protesting college student to a highly successful prosecutor in Philadelphia. And Jessie had started her own architectural firm. They were both members of the "establishment" that they'd railed against so vehemently in the 1960s. She watched the Clintons as they clapped in time with the music. *Then again, Bill and Hillary aren't that much different.*

"I can't see from back here."

Audrey glanced over at her partner of twenty-three years, amused at the frown that creased her forehead.

Jessie kept her hair neat and trim now, no longer sporting the locks that fell across her forehead in 1969. Quite a bit of gray was sprinkled throughout her dark tresses, more than what should be visible at forty-three. But she was just as hot and sexy as the night they met.

Jessie caught her staring. "What?"

"Nothing."

"You can't tell me you're not disappointed with where they stuck us. I thought we'd be up *there*." Jessie pointed emphatically toward the stage. When Audrey didn't respond, she said,

"Damn it, Audrey. We worked our asses off for him in Pennsylvania."

A tall blonde approached them and gripped Jessie's elbow. "Come on, babe. I can get you up front."

Audrey tried to remember where she'd seen her before, and recognition hit her fast—Elizabeth, one of the campaign workers from Pennsylvania. And she could never seem to keep her hands off Jessie.

Babe, Audrey mouthed as she caught Jessie's eye. Jessie shrugged.

Audrey hurried to keep up with them as Elizabeth shoved her way forward until they were four rows back from the stage.

Elizabeth draped her arm around Jessie's shoulders. "Don't they look great?"

Jessie quickly squirmed out of Elizabeth's embrace.

Elizabeth glanced over at Audrey. "Hey, didn't see you there."

Sure you didn't.

"What was your name again?" Elizabeth asked. "Allison?"

"Her name is Audrey, and she's my partner." Jessie pulled Audrey close.

Elizabeth waved dismissively. "Right. My fault." She turned her attention back to the stage. "We love you, Hillary!"

Hillary gave one of her open-mouthed grins and pointed at them. Hell, she could have been pointing at anyone within twenty feet of where they stood, but Audrey liked to believe she'd singled them out.

Jessie tugged her closer and kissed her cheek. "I love you."

Audrey's insecurities about Elizabeth's unexpected appearance melted away when she heard the emotion in Jessie's voice. More multicolored balloons fell around them from the rafters above. As another chorus of the Fleetwood Mac song began, she basked in the hope that sprang in her heart. Hope for the country's future if this man claimed the presidency in November. But much more than that—hope for their future. Just the two of them.

Audrey grabbed Jessie's hand. "Let's get out of here." She grinned at Jessie's look of surprise. "Hotel!" she shouted over the bedlam and pulled Jessie toward the exit.

They rode up the elevator in silence. Audrey studied the illuminated floors above the door as if they held all the answers to the world's troubles. Twenty-one…twenty-two…she felt Jessie's stare, and her mouth went dry.

The bell dinged, signaling their floor. Jessie walked in front of her down the hall to their room. Audrey admired the way the way her tailored suit showed off the tightness of her ass. Jessie slid the key card into the slot and held the door open for Audrey. Once she entered the room, she shut the door and clicked the dead bolt. Then she whirled around so fast, Audrey didn't have time to react. Jessie started unbuttoning Audrey's blouse.

"You look amazing in this. The blue brings out the blue in your eyes." She undid the last button and slowly slid the blouse off Audrey's shoulders. She pressed her lips against Audrey's neck as she rubbed her nipples through her camisole.

"Oh, god," Audrey whispered.

"But you look even more amazing with nothing on."

Audrey shuddered under Jessie's intense scrutiny. She quickly undressed. "Now you, babe." She emphasized the last word and reached for Jessie's jacket. Jessie grasped her hand to stop her.

"Elizabeth was being a bitch. I don't even like the woman. You know that, right?" Her dark eyes bored into Audrey's.

Audrey ducked her head.

"Hey," Jessie said softly. She tilted Audrey's chin up with

a tender touch of her finger. "I love you so much. You're the only woman for me. You have been since that magical night at Woodstock." She leaned forward and placed a light kiss on Audrey's lips. "I only see you." Jessie touched her own heart and then placed her hand above Audrey's left breast. "And my heart only belongs to you."

Audrey trembled with desire. "Make love to me, Jess. Please."

Jessie walked Audrey to the bed and pushed her gently onto the mattress. She never lost eye contact as she shed her clothes. Audrey's gaze raked over the sleek, muscled body that hadn't changed in their years together.

Jessie hovered over her. "You're as beautiful as the night we met."

She bent down and ran her tongue along Audrey's lips until Audrey opened her mouth and welcomed Jessie's searching tongue. Audrey moaned as Jessie softly caressed her breast and let her fingers drift down her body until she dipped into her wetness. Audrey arched into her touch, but Jessie stayed away from where Audrey craved her most.

Jessie continued the swirling movement of her fingers, kissing her way down Audrey's neck to her breasts, pausing to lavish each nipple with her tongue before moving lower...and lower.

Audrey willingly spread her legs. "Don't make me wait—" She hissed when Jessie's tongue dipped into her folds. Her hips jerked when Jessie reached her clit. In the next instant, she slid two fingers deep inside and began pumping in time with the rhythm of her feasting mouth.

Audrey felt her orgasm building, waiting to explode from her depths like a diver bursting through the water's surface in a frantic search of that first, precious breath of air.

Jessie tore her mouth away but kept up with the steady driving of her fingers. "Now, Audrey."

Hearing that plea from her lover sent Audrey flying over the edge. "Yesss!"

Jessie pushed into her until Audrey weakly stopped her hand. Jessie gently pulled out and leaned down to kiss away Audrey's tears. Her deep brown eyes shimmered with moisture. She started to speak, but Audrey placed a finger against her lips.

"I know, baby, I know," Audrey whispered.

New York State, August 17, 2009

They passed the *Welcome to New York* sign, but Audrey remained mute about where she was taking them for their fortieth anniversary. Jessie had a good guess, though. She reached across the gearshift and caressed Audrey's thigh. "This will be perfect."

Audrey briefly met Jessie's gaze and took her hand. "I didn't think I could keep the secret any longer once we got on I-87."

Jessie looked down at their joined hands and rubbed her thumb over Audrey's age spots.

"Not as young as we used to be, are we, hon?" Audrey grinned.

"I wouldn't want to be any other age than what I am today, and I wouldn't want anyone else but you these past forty years."

Audrey blinked a few times. "You always know just what to say."

"It's true."

They didn't speak anymore as their Sante Fe ate up the miles. Just before dusk, they reached their destination—the town of Bethel.

"You remember how to get to the field?" Jessie asked.

"Not exactly. But I checked it out online, and there's a marker to let us know we're in the right spot."

Jessie chuckled.

"What?" Audrey said as she made another turn.

"I think it's funny we're sixty now, and we have to look up directions. Remember when we would just get in our VW bug and drive, letting the road take us where it'd lead us?"

Audrey laughed. "Hey, we had to grow up a little."

She made a few more turns until they parked near a cement slab. They got out of the SUV and walked up to the marker to read the inscription. A breeze blew in from the west and ruffled Jessie's hair.

"I feel like we're on hallowed ground." Jessie spoke in a lowered voice as if she was afraid she'd disturb the ghosts of the rock stars who'd died since that remarkable time in music history.

"We are," Audrey said matter-of-factly. She turned to Jessie and smiled. A smile that still took Jessie's breath away. "It's where we met. The music was a bonus."

Jessie cupped her face. She placed a kiss on her lips that started out chaste, but quickly ignited something more. She pulled out of the kiss and rested her forehead against Audrey's. "You still do things to me, Audrey Cartwright."

"And that's a good thing, Jessie Roman." Audrey reached for Jessie's hand. "Come on. Let's walk down the fence line. I think I see where we first met."

Jessie laughed. "You can't possibly know that."

"So? It'll be close enough."

It had grown a little darker. Jessie stumbled once on the uneven ground, but Audrey caught her before she fell. They walked several more feet when Audrey suddenly stopped.

"Here. This is it."

"How do you know?" Jessie asked.

"Can't you just feel the energy?"

"Um...no. Not really."

Audrey reached into her fanny pack and pulled out a lighter... and what suspiciously looked like a joint.

"Where the hell did you get that?" Jessie said in shock.

"Never mind." She flicked the lighter and inhaled as she lit the joint. She held her breath and then exhaled. "Good shit, man."

"Do I know you?"

Audrey burst out laughing. "I wish you could see the look on your face. Here. Do *not* disappoint me, Jessie, and tell me you've gone all conservative."

Jessie glanced around them.

"There's no one here, silly. And who cares if there were."

"Well, I'd think you would, O Madam Prosecutor."

Audrey waved her hand. "It's just you and me and our memories."

Jessie took a hit. "Wow. That really *is* good shit."

They passed the joint back and forth until it was down to nothing. Audrey pressed it against the heel of her boot to extinguish it completely. She cocked her head. "Do you hear that?"

Jessie strained to hear any sound but the chirping of the crickets. "No."

Audrey took her hand, spun Jessie around in front of her and wrapped her arms around Jessie's waist in an embrace that felt like an old friend. "I think I hear Janis."

A warm and mellow feeling washing over her, Jessie leaned her head back on Audrey's shoulder. "You do?"

"Mmm-hmm. And I think she's singing our song." Audrey nuzzled her ear. "Can you hear it?"

Jessie closed her eyes as Audrey hummed "Try (Just a Little Bit Harder)" while unsnapping Jessie's jeans. Jessie stiffened in her arms.

"This is where I say, no one can see." Audrey pulled the zipper down in tantalizing slowness and pushed Jessie's panties aside.

"Oh, my, you're just as wet, too, aren't you?" Audrey nibbled Jessie's neck as she started stroking Jessie's clit. "Listen to her voice, Jess. Let it fill your senses."

Jessie moaned with each stroke of Audrey's fingers.

"You are so, so hard. You're ready, aren't you?"

Jessie nodded.

Audrey pinched Jessie's nipple and strummed Jessie's clit until she came in a rush.

"Oh, god," Jessie cried, gripping Audrey's arms to keep from collapsing onto the ground.

"I've got you, baby, and I'm never letting you go."

Jessie's breathing finally returned to normal. Audrey pulled her hand from Jessie's panties, and Jessie turned in her arms to kiss the only woman she'd ever loved.

"Happy anniversary, Audrey," she murmured against her lips.

Audrey smiled. "Here's to another forty years of magic."

HOMECOMING

Kathleen Tudor

Chelsea's phone alarm rang out in the dark of early morning, and she rolled over to shut it off. She started this day like she always did, with a shock of dread that hit her like cold water breaking over her head. She lay in the silent dark, staring at the ceiling for a few minutes, wondering if today the tears would fail to find her. But they welled up right on cue, spilling over as she wept silently, squeezing out the terror and the nightmares and the hopeless thoughts and making room for what needed to be done.

She'd started setting her alarm ten minutes early after the first month, when she realized that the tears were going to be a daily inconvenience—an incontrovertible fact of life. Now, as the last of the tears left her, she blew her nose and turned on the light, getting ready for her day. She washed her face, got dressed and only then allowed herself the daily jolt of hope as she loaded her email. Sometimes it would be days or even terrible weeks between the times that Jessica could write to her, but she looked for her messages every morning, regardless.

Today, hope was realized. The message sat at the top of her inbox, automatically starred and marked as important by the filters she'd added to her account, and she took a deep breath to keep from screaming in joy. She loved to savor the moments before she opened the emails, letting the joy of hearing from Jessica wash over her. Jessica was alive. She was well. She was reaching out across the ocean from a place of danger to the heart of her home—reaching for Chelsea.

Chelsea closed her eyes and sought that connection, almost tangible to her during these long months. Then she took another deep breath, no longer able to contain the smile that split her face and threatened to make her cheeks ache, and clicked on the email.

It was short, only a couple of sentences, but it was the best thing she had seen in the eleven months and four days since Jessica had been deployed.

Ten more days, my love. Hang on. Be strong. I'm coming home.

The next ten days passed in a blur. Chelsea still had her job to do, and she refused to be distracted from teaching her seventh-grade English course, even when she was so full of emotions that she thought she would burst.

At home, she spent days scrubbing the house from top to bottom, and although she had kept it neat before, now it shone from every corner. She tried to find a chore or a paper to grade or a meal to make and freeze to fill every spare second, or she was sure she would go crazy with the waiting, the wondering and the worrying.

And then, like magic, ten days had finally flown by and she was at the airport, dancing from one foot to the other and checking the arrivals board every few seconds as if it could hurry Jessica along. She would have given anything to wait at the gate, but airport security was unmoved by her pleas, so she waited anxiously at the baggage carousel.

She was looking at the arrivals screen again—her heart pounding so hard she could hardly hear anything else around her—when the first rush of people from Jessica's flight poured through the gate. She stepped forward, moved up onto her toes, strained her eyes searching back and forth...*Jessica.*

She was in the middle of the pack, but she quickly moved to one side as if she knew that Chelsea would need a clear path. Because she certainly did. Chelsea took off at a dead run, all of the careful discipline of the last year forgotten in her unbridled joy. She nearly knocked Jessica off her feet when they collided, and she leapt into her wife's arms.

Jessica laughed and squeezed Chelsea until she could hardly breathe, and Chelsea stifled tears, clutching at Jessica's olive drabs as if she couldn't believe she had really come home at last. When they both stopped babbling and touching one another long enough to look around them, they realized they had an audience. Some people passed, sniffing in disdain, but others smiled and even winked at the women, or nodded encouragingly. One old man stopped and put his hand out, and Jessica shook it, nodding gravely before he moved past.

"Come on," Jessica whispered. "I just want you, and home."

Chelsea waited while Jessica retrieved her duffel, then led the way to the car. Neither of them could speak on the ride home. Jessica sat in the passenger seat staring at Chelsea, and it was difficult for Chelsea to keep her eyes on the road. She longed to say something, but how could she convey the love, the longing and the fear of the last months? How could she tell Jessica that she was terrified and so proud her heart could just about burst every day? She wasn't sure if these were things that could ever be spoken, so she choked on them instead, lost for words.

When they pulled into the driveway, Chelsea turned the car off and sat, both hands on the wheel, the words bursting from her throat as if she had no control over them. "I *missed* you," she said, and then the dam burst in earnest and she did what she'd sworn not to do and sobbed as if her heart was being torn out of her.

Jessica leaned over and pulled Chelsea toward her, cradling her head against her breasts and brushing her hair back as she murmured soothing noises. Chelsea clutched at the uniform as sobs racked her. "I've ruined it. I'm sorry," she managed to say in between sobs, but Jessica only continued to shush her gently, brushing her hair away from her face and rocking her in the confines of the car.

When Chelsea had calmed, Jessica got out and went around the car, opening the driver's door to help Chelsea out. "I know you must have been so scared for me," she said, pulling Chelsea into her arms. Chelsea felt like a child, weak and helpless, and she wrapped her arms around her wife as if she would never let go of her again. "I know. I know how scared you must have been. You haven't ruined anything, Chel. This is exactly what I wanted, all year. I just wanted to hold you and make you feel better, and now I can."

"I tried to be brave..." If Chelsea had thought she'd lost control before, she was in for a surprise. She broke down, nearly collapsing and blinded by the tears that suddenly flowed from her like a river.

"You are brave," Jessica whispered, over and over. "So brave." Chelsea felt herself being lifted up, like she was floating in a river of tears, and all she had to anchor her to the world was her grip on Jessica's olive drabs and the smell of her lover's hair.

She wasn't sure how long it was before the shuddering sobs stopped and she was able to peel her eyes open. They were in the living room, Jessica on the couch and Chelsea draped over her lap. "I missed you," she said again, and this time the words came more easily.

"I missed you, too." And then Jessica kissed her, and Chelsea's world tilted yet again. A whole year with no kisses, unless you counted that frantic greeting at the airport—a whole year without Jessica's soft mouth on hers, without the way she nibbled at Chelsea's upper lip, without the sigh she made when Chelsea licked sweetly at her lips.

Chelsea had thought she'd be in a hurry when Jessica finally came home, but she realized now that she had all the time in the world to give her hero a proper welcome. And Jessica seemed in no hurry, either, letting the kiss linger and their tongues dance as she ran her hands over what she could reach of Chelsea's body. They stayed in a humming, pleased clutch for what could have been hours, letting their kisses convey all the loss and longing and love they'd both wanted to share for months.

"Let's go to bed," Chelsea whispered, and Jessica braced herself, then pushed up, standing with Chelsea still in her arms. They both giggled, and Jessica carried her to the bedroom.

When she set her down on the bed, Chelsea reached up and caught at her dog tags, bringing Jessica down on top of her amidst more giggles. Their hands started to roam, exploring bodies that had gone too long without each other. Chelsea thought she had gained some weight and still wasn't sure she liked the little extra bulges that came with the extra curves. Jessica, on the other hand, had lost any fat she might once have carried, becoming leaner and harder with occasional havens of surprising softness.

"You look amazing," Chelsea said, easing her hand inside

Jessica's fatigue shirt. Jessica shrugged it off, tossing it and her bra aside so that her upper body was bare to Chelsea's exploring fingers. "You have a new scar." She tickled a spot along Jessica's ribs.

"They were shooting at a jeep I was working on. I didn't even know I'd gotten hurt until we got back to the base. It was just a tiny piece of shrapnel," she said, and Chelsea looked at the half-inch scar and tried to pretend she believed her.

Chelsea pulled her blouse off, and Jessica popped the clasp on her bra before she could reach for it. Next came Jessica's heavy boots and Chelsea's soft pair of flats, and then they were wrapped around one another, pulling each other close and continuing their earlier kiss with enough passion and heat to set the bed on fire. Their legs tangled as if they couldn't possibly get close enough, and Jessica reached down, pushing Chelsea's skirt out of the way and reaching into her panties to find her hot, wet center.

Chelsea arched as the first electric touch shot through her, then moaned as her lover's gentle fingers explored and aroused her, pushing her quickly toward the brink. She panted, gasped and let out a long, low keen as pleasure coursed through her, ripping away the last vestiges of pain and loneliness with them.

When her breathing returned to normal, she reached into the nightstand and pulled out a toy that hadn't seen the light of day in a year. "Want to ride?" she asked, a shy smile on her face as she held up the double dildo. Jessica smiled, kicking out of her fatigues and reaching to help Chelsea out of her skirt. Naked like this, Chelsea thought that Jessica looked so vulnerable and sweetly feminine, no trace remaining of the solid soldier except the strict updo and the tiredness around eyes that had seen too much.

Chelsea waited for Jessica to lie back, then teased at the edges of her lips with the dildo, coating it in Jessica's juices. She lifted it to her own mouth, watching Jessica's eyes dilate as she licked the cream away from the head of the toy. "I've missed that taste."

"Plenty more time for that. Right now I want you," Jessica said, and Chelsea answered by returning the dildo to her lover's cunt and pushing it slowly past her inner lips, fucking her deeper and deeper with every thrust. Jessica let her head fall back, and a small moan escaped her as the dildo settled deeply into her body. The other cock head protruded from her, and Chelsea straddled her wife, guided the dildo to her center and began to slowly lower herself onto it.

Jessica moaned again as the added pressure pushed the dildo deeper into her body. She pushed back, and it was Chelsea's turn to moan as she sank toward her lover's body. As soon as the dildo was all the way inside her, Chelsea lay down atop her wife and kissed her deeply. "Welcome home," she whispered. Then she rocked her hips forward, making both of them gasp, and soon they were both rocking and bucking against one another, crying out in a sensual chorus as they drove themselves and each other to greater heights of pleasure.

They came together, Jessica's voice deep and joyful as she rocked with her orgasm, and Chelsea's a sweet gasp. She couldn't get enough air to cry out. She shuddered, her whole body convulsing with pleasure, magnified when she felt Jessica quivering beneath her. They remained that way, tangled together, for a long time, running their hands over one another and pressing kisses wherever they could reach.

When they finally rolled apart, Chelsea reached for her phone. "What are you doing?" Jessica asked.

"Resetting my alarm," Chelsea answered, setting the phone back on the table and curling up into Jessica's arms. "I don't need to get up so early anymore."

YOU DON'T BRING ME FLOWERS

Radclyffe

Dr. Pearce Rifkin leaned into the doorway of the OR office and waited while the nurse on the desk finished giving an update to the receptionist in the family waiting area. As soon as she hung up, Pearce said, "What's going on in room seven? They were supposed to be ready for me an hour ago."

"Hold on." The nurse switched screens on the small monitor tucked into the corner above her workstation, and Pearce angled her head to survey the activity in the operating room. Equipment and at least half a dozen people crowded around the operating table, obscuring the patient. He was only a shapeless mound beneath sterile green drapes. She frowned. "Is that Rappaport? What's he doing in there?"

"They called for him half an hour ago. Apparently they found something with the kidney they wanted him to check."

Pearce glanced at the big round clock on the wall. Three forty-five. She had to be done by six. "Look, call me as soon as they're ready. I'll be in the office."

"Will do," the nurse said, her attention already elsewhere.

Pearce cut through the pre-op holding area, skirted the row of gurneys waiting for patients to leave recovery and slapped the palm-sized red button on the wall to open the double doors leading to the hall. Friday afternoon—always the same. Unexpected admissions, traumas, add-on cases. Delay after delay. She knew planning anything for Friday night was risky, but what choice did she have? Wynter was on call Saturday. Sunday was out—Wynter would be tired—and getting a sitter would be harder. Besides, anniversaries were supposed to be celebrated on the day, not some random who-knew-when-they'd-ever-have-time point in the future. And this was a big anniversary—six months since the baby was born. Six amazing, incredible months. Being a parent was completely unlike anything she'd expected—at turns exhilarating and terrifying. He was so little—perfect in every way, but so helpless. The responsibility and wonder were enormous, and from the moment she'd held him and looked into Wynter's exhausted but exultant eyes, everything had changed. She'd thought she'd loved Wynter as much as she possibly could, but in that instant, she loved her in a way she hadn't known possible. With reverence, with a soul-deep need that kept her awake at night, wondering how she could possibly do without either one of them.

She punched the button on the elevator and glanced at her watch. Four P.M. "Damn it."

"Hey, Pearce," a familiar voice said. "You look like I feel. What's going on?"

"Hey, Ali," Pearce said to the other surgeon and her wife's best friend. "I'm just waiting around to do triple tubes on the MVA from this afternoon. *Waiting* being the operative word."

"Typical Friday, huh?"

Pearce watched the numbers slowly tick down as the elevator

approached. "Yeah. Figures I'd get hung up when I've got plans."

"Anything to do with the special delivery to the trauma unit this morning?"

Pearce grinned. "Maybe."

"Come on, spill."

The elevator doors opened, Pearce said "Sorry" to the occupants and let it pass. "You won't tell her, will you?"

"Not a word. The flowers were gorgeous. Wynter was speechless."

Pearce leaned against the wall and sighed. "I should have sent them a lot sooner."

"What's the occasion?"

"Nate is six months old today."

Ali's dark eyes sparkled. "Oh, my god. So fast. I have to get my godson a present. So—Wynter gets flowers on Nate's half-birthday because...?"

"She's been juggling a lot since he was born—taking care of him, work, studying for her boards. She needs a break." Pearce ran a hand through her hair. "We need a break."

"Everything okay?" Ali asked gently.

"Oh yeah. It's just—crazy, you know? And I don't think..." Pearce sighed. "I don't think I tell her enough how great she is."

Ali smiled. "She's really happy, you know. You must be doing something right."

"Well, I've got a big evening planned—I sent the invitation with the flowers."

"Uh-huh. Still waiting for details."

"I just told her to dress for dinner so I could keep the rest a surprise. I reserved a private dining suite at the Four Seasons. The sitter is coming at seven, and we've got five hours all to ourselves."

"Wow. Nice date." Ali grinned.

"It's the first time we've had a chance to get away since he was born." Pearce glanced at her watch. "If I get this case done."

"I hope you make it." Ali sketched a wave as the elevator doors opened again and Pearce stepped inside.

"Me too." Pearce squeezed past a stretcher bearing an elderly patient, who snored softly, and settled in the corner as the elevator descended. She'd wanted everything to be perfect. Wynter had taken a month off after Nate was born, and since she'd been back to work, they'd both been so busy with him and their hospital schedules she sometimes felt like she never saw her. When she did, they were both so tired all they could do was make sure the baby was taken care of before they fell into bed, only to get up a few hours later for a feeding, grab a couple more hours' sleep and then head back to the hospital. She just missed her, and tonight was supposed to be just them, a chance to reconnect.

An hour later she was still waiting. She called the OR. "Gloria, it's Rifkin. Can you get me an ETA for room seven?"

She listened to silence for a minute and then the night-shift nurse came on. "They said at least another hour—maybe. Rappaport is taking out that kidney."

"Thanks." Pearce disconnected, rubbed both hands over her face and picked up the phone to call home. "Hi, babe," she said when Wynter answered. "I'm still here waiting on that trauma patient. It's looking like a couple of hours."

"You're not going to make it, are you?" Wynter sighed.

"I'm so sorry. If I'm not too late, we could still—"

"Hey, I understand." Wynter paused. "The sitter will be here in a few minutes. I'll just tell her we don't need her and pay her for travel time. We'll try again some other time."

"Wynter—"

"It's okay, really. I've got to be in early tomorrow anyhow."

"Okay, babe. I'll see you later then."

"Take it easy, honey."

Pearce disconnected, hung up the phone and switched off the desk light. Leaning back in her chair, she closed her eyes. At least she'd sent Wynter flowers. A dozen multicolored daisies—her favorites. She always meant to send her flowers just for no reason, but life always seemed to get in the way.

She listened to her secretary Angela moving around in the cubicle outside her office and then the light shining underneath her door went out. Everyone would have left the offices by now. She probably should work, but dictating charts wasn't her favorite thing to do under the best of circumstances. She wasn't in the mood now. She thought about stretching out on the couch and grabbing a nap, and was about to get up when the door opened and Wynter stepped inside.

Pearce sat up straight, her hands flat on the desk, her heart suddenly pounding. "Hi."

"Hi," Wynter said. "I saw Angela in the hall. She said you were in here. Why are you sitting in the dark?"

"Just thinking." The only light in the room came through the window behind her, the reflection of the halogen lights from the ER parking area slanting across the space between them, illuminating Wynter's elegant profile with such delicacy she appeared like a dream apparition suddenly come to life. "What are you doing here?"

"I wanted to tell you I liked the flowers."

"I'm sorry about tonight."

Wynter reached behind her and turned the lock on the door. Pearce's mouth went dry as Wynter shrugged out of her long wool coat, draped it on a chair and walked toward her. She was wearing a dress she hadn't worn since before she'd gotten pregnant—a red silk scoop-necked sheath that clung to her curves and stopped mid-thigh.

"Is that what you were planning on wearing tonight?"

"For the first part of the evening." Wynter gripped the arms of Pearce's chair and pushed it far enough away from the desk that she could settle into Pearce's lap. She wrapped her arms around Pearce's neck and kissed her. "Then I planned on you taking it off."

Pearce's head started to pound. She skimmed her hand up Wynter's thigh and under the hem of the dress. "I love you in this dress."

"You'd better love me in anything." Wynter nipped at Pearce's lower lip.

"I love you out of it too." Pearce kissed Wynter's throat and buried her face in the curve of her neck, tightening inside as she inhaled Wynter's distinctive sunshine-and-spice scent. She groaned softly. "You feel so good."

Wynter tugged Pearce's scrub shirt out of her pants and pressed her palm against Pearce's stomach. "This is just a preview because I know you don't have much time."

"Wynter," Pearce murmured, rubbing her cheek over the inner curve of Wynter's breast above the red crescent of silk. "I love you."

"I know." Wynter snagged the tie on Pearce's scrub pants and pulled. "I loved the flowers. And the date night."

"I wanted to do something special."

Wynter slid her hand into Pearce's scrubs and laughed softly. "Commando, Doctor Rifkin?"

Pearce caressed the outer curve of Wynter's thigh, the silk teasing over her bare forearm as she stroked higher. She found only soft, warm skin. "You too."

"Just being practical." Wynter sighed and shifted, parting

her thighs. "I've been thinking about your hands on me since I got your invitation."

Pearce traced the seam between Wynter's thigh and belly to the soft curls at the apex of her thighs. She slowly brushed the base of her clitoris and Wynter gasped, thrusting her hips. Pearce kissed the pulse hammering in Wynter's throat. "I've been thinking about this for weeks."

"I'm sorry I haven't—"

"No. It's okay," Pearce said. "I just...need you."

Wynter covered Pearce's hand, the red silk a whisper between their skin, and pressed Pearce's fingers deeper between her thighs. She was wet and warm and open. "I need you too. Always."

Pearce slipped deeper, cupping her inside and out. Wynter gave a tiny cry and closed her fingers around Pearce's clitoris. Pearce's stomach jumped. She didn't have long. Tightening her arm around Wynter's waist, she stroked between her legs. Wynter followed her lead, her caresses growing harder, more erratic as her hips rose and fell, riding Pearce's fingers.

"I'm going to come, baby," Wynter warned breathlessly. "Baby, I'm going to come."

"Don't hold back," Pearce gasped, pressing deeper, her clitoris tingling, the explosion starting. "With you."

Wynter arched in her lap, her thighs tightening around Pearce's hand, holding her inside. The pounding pulse of Wynter's flesh echoed the thunder in Pearce's head. She pressed her mouth to Wynter's breast, shuddering as the storm consumed her.

Laughing, Wynter collapsed against Pearce's shoulder. "God, I love making you come."

"Ditto."

"You'll have to change your scrubs."

"Luckily I have a stash in the closet."

"You okay?"

"Never better." Pearce dropped her head back and smiled. "Never been happier in my life."

"Me neither." Wynter kissed her again and stood, straightening her dress. "See you at home?"

"Replay?"

"That's a promise." Wynter tapped a fingertip to Pearce's mouth. "And, baby, you don't even have to send me flowers. They're beautiful, but all I need is you."

ABOUT THE AUTHORS

CHEYENNE BLUE (www.cheyenneblue.com) has lived in the United States, Ireland, the UK and Switzerland, but she still calls Australia home. Her erotica has appeared in many anthologies, including *Best Women's Erotica*, *Mammoth Best New Erotica*, *Best Lesbian Erotica* and *Best Lesbian Romance*.

Called a "legendary erotica heavy-hitter" (by the über-legendary Violet Blue), **ANDREA DALE** (www.cyvarwydd.com) dedicates "Sepia Showers" to mothers and daughters everywhere. Her work has appeared in about 100 anthologies from Harlequin Spice, Avon Red and Cleis Press, and is available online at Soul's Road Press.

KIKI DELOVELY is a queer femme performer/writer whose work has appeared in *Best Lesbian Erotica 2011* and *2012*, *Salacious* magazine, *Gotta Have It: 69 Stories of Sudden Sex*, *Take Me There: Transgender and Genderqueer Erotica* and *Say Please: Lesbian BDSM Erotica*.

ROWAN ELIZABETH (www.rowanelizabeth.com) has been published over three dozen times in works by Cleis Press, Susie Bright and Rachel Kramer Bussel.

DENA HANKINS writes from her sailboat, wherever she may be moored, has coached thousands of couples on keeping the home fires burning while working at a feminist sex toy shop and is fifteen years into her own dream relationship.

STELLA HARRIS (www.stellaharris.net) has been getting off to erotic fiction since she found her mother's stash when she was twelve years old. When she's not reading or writing smut she loves to travel, bake, garden and talk to strangers on the Internet.

JAY LAWRENCE is an expatriate Scot who currently hangs out near Vancouver, Canada. She is the author of over a dozen erotic novels and many short stories that have appeared in publications on both sides of the Atlantic.

D. JACKSON LEIGH (www.djacksonleigh.com) grew up barefoot and happy, swimming in farm ponds and riding rude ponies. Her most recent novel, *Touch Me Gently*, is a romantic tale of betrayal and family secrets set among the shaded tobacco fields of south Georgia.

SOMMER MARSDEN (sommermarsden.blogspot.com) is the author of *Hard Lessons*, *Base Nature*, *Lucky 13* and *I'm on Fire*. Her shorts have appeared in dozens of anthologies including *Best Women's Erotica 2009*, *2010* and *2011*, *Eat Me*, *The Mammoth Book of Threesomes and Moresomes*, *Where the Girls Are* and *Best Lesbian Romance 2011*.

ANNA MEADOWS is a part-time executive assistant, part-time Sapphic housewife. Her work appears in eleven Cleis Press anthologies and on the Lambda Literary Foundation website.

After years of living in England and Israel, **CATHERINE PAULSSEN** now enjoys the magic and excitement of her new hometown Berlin, where she works as a freelancer and dedicates every spare minute to writing erotica.

CHRIS PAYNTER is an editor and an author. Her recent works include the *Playing for First* baseball series.

RACHEL RANDALL's (rachelrandall.wordpress.com) erotic romance draws inspiration from the kinky, classy cool of London. She loves to create characters who know what they want and how to ask for it (usually with a slow slide down to their knees).

LARKIN ROSE (larkinrose.weebly.com) lives in a "blink and you've missed it" town in the beautiful state of South Carolina with her partner, Rose (hence the pen name), a portion of their seven brats, a chunky grandson and too many animals to name.

DEREK SHANNON is an expat American now living in the north of England, an unabashed Trekkie from Kirk's days. His previous published works include *Slave Hunt, Bound Over* and *In Hot Pursuit.*

KATHLEEN TUDOR (polyspace.wordpress.com) is a writer, editor, a lesbian, a wife, a mother and a knitter. Her work has appeared in *Like That Spark*, *Best Bondage 2012*, *Hot Under the Collar* and other anthologies.

REBEKAH WEATHERSPOON was raised in southern New Hampshire and now lives in southern California with an individual who is much more tech savvy than she will ever be. Her novels include *Better Off Red, The Fling* and *Blacker than Blue.*

ABOUT THE EDITOR

RADCLYFFE (www.radfic.com) has written more than forty romance novels, edited over a dozen anthologies, and presented numerous writing workshops in the United States and abroad. She is an eight-time finalist and three-time winner of the Lambda Literary Award, and a recipient of RWA FF&P Prism, RWA FTHRW Lories Best Published Mainstream novel, and IPPY awards. A member of the Saints and Sinners Literary Hall of Fame, she is also the president and publisher of Bold Strokes Books. Her 2012 novels include *Night Hunt*, written as L.L. Raand, the third in the Midnight Hunters paranormal romance series, the First Responders novel *Oath of Honor,* and *Crossroads,* a medical romance.

More of the Best Lesbian Romance

Buy 4 books, Get 1 *FREE**

Best Lesbian Romance 2013
Edited by Radclyffe

Radclyffe, the *Best Lesbian Romance* series legendary editor and a bestselling romance writer herself, says it best: "Love and romance may defy simple definition, but every story in this collection speaks to the universal thread that binds lovers everywhere—possibility."
ISBN 978-1-57344-901-4 $15.95

Best Lesbian Romance 2012
Edited by Radclyffe

Best Lesbian Romance 2012 celebrates the dizzying sensation of falling in love—and the electrifying thrill of sexual passion. Romance maestra Radclyffe gathers irresistible stories of lesbians in love to awaken your desire and send your imagination soaring.
ISBN 978-1-57344-757-7 $14.95

Best Lesbian Romance 2011
Edited by Radclyffe

"*Best Lesbian Romance* series editor Radclyffe has assembled a respectable crop of 17 authors for this year's offering. The stories are diverse in tone, style and subject, each containing a satisfying, surprising twist."—*Curve*
ISBN 978-1-57344-427-9 $14.95

Best Lesbian Romance 2010
Edited by Radclyffe

Ranging from the short and ever-so-sweet to the recklessly passionate, *Best Lesbian Romance 2010* is essential reading for anyone who favors the highly imaginative, the deeply sensual, and the very loving.
ISBN 978-1-57344-376-0 $14.95

Best Lesbian Romance 2009
Edited by Radclyffe

Scale the heights of emotion and the depths of desire with this collection of the very best lesbian romance writing of the year.
ISBN 978-1-57344-333-3 $14.95

*** Free book of equal or lesser value. Shipping and applicable sales tax extra.**
Cleis Press • (800) 780-2279 • orders@cleispress.com
www.cleispress.com

Fuel Your Fantasies

Buy 4 books, Get 1 *FREE**

Carnal Machines
Steampunk Erotica
Edited by D. L. King

In this decadent fusing of technology and romance, outstanding contemporary erotica writers use the enthralling possibilities of the 19th-century steam age to tease and titillate.

ISBN 978-1-57344-654-9 $14.95

The Sweetest Kiss
Ravishing Vampire Erotica
Edited by D. L. King

These sanguine tales give new meaning to the term "dead sexy" and feature beautiful bloodsuckers whose desires go far beyond blood.

ISBN 978-1-57344-371-5 $15.95

The Handsome Prince
Gay Erotic Romance
Edited by Neil Plakcy

A bawdy collection of bedtime stories brimming with classic fairy tale characters, reimagined and recast for any man who has dreamt of the day his prince will come. These sexy stories fuel fantasies and remind us all of the power of true romance.

ISBN 978-1-57344-659-4 $14.95

Daughters of Darkness
Lesbian Vampire Tales
Edited by Pam Keesey

"A tribute to the sexually aggressive woman and her archetypal roles, from nurturing goddess to dangerous predator."
—*The Advocate*

ISBN 978-1-57344-233-6 $14.95

Dark Angels
Lesbian Vampire Erotica
Edited by Pam Keesey

Dark Angels collects tales of lesbian vampires, the quintessential bad girls, archetypes of passion and terror. These tales of desire are so sharply erotic you'll swear you've been bitten!

ISBN 978-1-57344-252-7 $13.95

*** Free book of equal or lesser value. Shipping and applicable sales tax extra.**
Cleis Press • (800) 780-2279 • orders@cleispress.com
www.cleispress.com

More of the Best Lesbian Erotica

Buy 4 books, Get 1 *FREE**

Sometimes She Lets Me
Best Butch/Femme Erotica
Edited by Tristan Taormino

Does the swagger of a confident butch make you swoon? Do your knees go weak when you see a femme straighten her stockings? In *Sometimes She Lets Me,* Tristan Taormino chooses her favorite butch/femme stories from the *Best Lesbian Erotica* series.
ISBN 978-1-57344-382-1 $14.95

Lesbian Lust
Erotic Stories
Edited by Sacchi Green

Lust: It's the engine that drives us wild on the way to getting us off, and lesbian lust is the heart, soul and red-hot core of this anthology.
ISBN 978-1-57344-403-3 $14.95

Girl Crush
Women's Erotic Fantasies
Edited by R. Gay

In the steamy stories of *Girl Crush,* women satisfy their curiosity about the erotic possibilities of their infatuations.
ISBN 978-1-57344-394-4 $14.95

Girl Crazy
Coming Out Erotica
Edited by Sacchi Green

These irresistible stories of first times of all kinds invite the reader to savor that delicious, dizzy feeling known as "girl crazy."
ISBN 978-1-57344-352-4 $14.95

Lesbian Cowboys
Erotic Adventures
Edited by Sacchi Green and Rakelle Valencia

With stories that are edgy as shiny spurs and tender as broken-in leather, fifteen first-rate writers share their take on an iconic fantasy.
ISBN 978-1-57344-361-6 $14.95

*** Free book of equal or lesser value. Shipping and applicable sales tax extra.**
Cleis Press • (800) 780-2279 • orders@cleispress.com
www.cleispress.com

Essential Lesbian Erotica

Buy 4 books, Get 1 *FREE**

The Harder She Comes
Butch/Femme Erotica
Edited by D. L. King

Some butches worship at the altar of their femmes, and many adorable girls long for the embrace of their suave, sexy daddies. In *The Harder She Comes*, we meet femmes who salivate at the sight of packed jeans and bois who dream of touching the corseted waist of a beautiful, confident woman.
ISBN 978-1-57344-778-2 $14.95

Girls Who Bite
Lesbian Vampire Erotica
Edited by Delilah Devlin

Whether depicting a traditional blood-drinker seducing a meal, a psychic vampire stealing the life force of an unknowing host, or a real-life sanguinarian seeking a partner to share a ritual bloodletting, the stories in *Girls Who Bite* are a sensual surprise.
ISBN 978-1-57344-715-7 $14.95

Girls Who Score
Hot Lesbian Erotica
Edited by Ily Goyanes

Girl jocks always manage to see a lot of action off the field. *Girls Who Score* is a winner, filled with story after story of competitive, intriguing women engaging in all kinds of contact sports.
ISBN 978-1-57344-825-3 $15.95

Wild Girls, Wild Nights
True Lesbian Sex Stories
Edited by Sacchi Green

Forget those fabled urban myths of lesbians who fill up U-Hauls on the second date and lead sweetly romantic lives of cocoa and comfy slippers. These are tales of wild women with dirty minds, untamed tongues and the occasional cuff or clamp. And they're all true!
ISBN 978-1-57344-933-5 $15.95

Stripped Down
Lesbian Sex Stories
Edited by Tristan Taormino

Where else but in a Tristan Taormino erotica collection can you find a femme vigilante, a virgin baby butch and a snake handler jostling for attention? The salacious stories in *Stripped Down* will draw you in and sweep you off your feet.
ISBN 978-1-57344-794-2 $15.95

*** Free book of equal or lesser value. Shipping and applicable sales tax extra.**
Cleis Press • (800) 780-2279 • orders@cleispress.com
www.cleispress.com

Ordering is easy! Call us toll free or fax us to place your MC/VISA order.
You can also mail the order form below with payment to:
Cleis Press, 2246 Sixth St., Berkeley, CA 94710.

ORDER FORM

QTY	TITLE	PRICE

SUBTOTAL	
SHIPPING	
SALES TAX	
TOTAL	

Add $3.95 postage/handling for the first book ordered and $1.00 for each additional book. Outside North America, please contact us for shipping rates. California residents add 9% sales tax. Payment in U.S. dollars only.

* Free book of equal or lesser value. Shipping and applicable sales tax extra.

Cleis Press • Phone: (800) 780-2279 • Fax: (510) 845-8001
orders@cleispress.com • www.cleispress.com
You'll find more great books on our website

Follow us on Twitter @cleispress • Friend/fan us on Facebook

Printed in the United States
By Bookmasters